A Curse of Silver

For Grandma, whose story I carry with me every day.

CHAPTER ONE

When the castle's tower finally toppled to the ground, the smells of singed pages and flesh wafted on the breeze. She felt the impact in the marrow of her bones, but she couldn't stop running.

How the morning sun could shine on such a thing, she didn't care to know.

She knew without having to see their red banners that the mage hunters were here. The fires were their weapon of choice for an infestation of magic.

Smoke laced her lungs. Kitchen staff and castle servants tore past her.

No one stopped Everin to tell her she was going the wrong way.

Her stomach twisted, and she could feel the mashed corn she'd taken from the kitchen for last night's dinner start to rise in her throat.

This is all because of you.

In the last few weeks, she'd taken to talking to herself as if she could divide into more than one person. As if she could dissect this new part of her from the rest.

Even though it hurt to breathe, Everin didn't stop running until she slammed against the latch door of the stables. As her fingers fumbled with the metal, she exhaled to find that it wasn't yet hot.

Maybe her luck would hold further. Maybe someone else had freed the stabled horses once the fire had started to spread through the castle. She passed inside the barn in a blur.

Panicked screams clawed through the air. The horses were still here.

At once, her hands flew from stall door to stall door, flinging them open as black, brown, and gray shapes moved about in the confined spaces. They whinnied as they raced past her.

Her blood throbbed inside her veins, and acrid smoke smeared her nostrils. The fire was getting closer.

She *knew* he was here. She had to get to him.

Even though her thoughts ran wild inside her, her hands were steady as she came to the metal latch of the last stall.

Where is he? He isn't …

"Tracker?"

The stall door swung wide, and Everin's knees nearly buckled. Tracker's white-tipped nose pushed against her throat, and warmth and moisture coated her skin. Unlike his neighbors, he didn't bolt at the first opportunity to escape the disaster approaching.

Even so, Tracker's tail swished enough to slam itself against the wood of his stall. An eye as black as a beetle's shell watched her.

Before she'd switched to a job inside the castle, she'd been responsible for cleaning their stalls. Tracker knew her secrets like no one else—never mind that he was a horse.

They both needed to get far away from the burning castle. Even if she couldn't take Tracker with her—wherever she was supposed to go *now*—she wanted him to be safe.

But, gods, she couldn't think about the kind of future that was before her. Or rather, the lack of one.

She had thought she could live out her life here, undetected. Even if that meant she was to be alone.

A noise at the other end of the stables turned her stomach. For too many precious seconds, she couldn't move.

They've come. They're here.

They've found me.

It was less a decision and more an instinct. Everin dove to the corner of Tracker's stall where she'd been sleeping unnoticed for months now.

Like a good boy, Tracker didn't rear up or whinny at the movement. Everin kept one hand near his flank, not daring a whisper.

They were silent as boot steps echoed hollowly in the barn.

Everin's other hand tightened into a fist. But her eyes fell on her companion.

I can't risk trying it. It could hurt him.

It was the *thing* that was within the part of her that she imagined she could cleave off. She thought of it like an infection, contained to only a part of her body. For now.

It had only appeared a few months ago. Everin had been foolish to think that she could hide the signs.

Her breath staled in her throat.

A shadow had fallen across the stall.

"Calm, boy. It's only a saddle."

Everin couldn't think anymore. She knew that voice. And it wasn't any mage hunter.

Everin was already on her knees, so she couldn't go any lower. Even so, it felt disrespectful to address him from where she was.

"My sire—"

Prince Alaric turned his gaze on her. From where she squatted among damp straw, she could see the gold of his eyes, his lashes brushing against each other as they beheld her in the rough-spun dress that she'd been wearing for several days. Once, the garment had been a pretty shade of wildflower blue. It was gray now.

But what he said next froze her racing heart.

"You're here." His golden eyes, the trait passed down by his royal lineage, didn't blink as they took her in. The prince's mouth lifted at one corner as he murmured, "I should have known."

Everin hadn't moved since he'd seen her. She didn't think she'd breathed, either.

Her voice came out hoarse. "You must've mistaken me for someone else, your Highness."

Everin washed plates and cutlery in the castle kitchens. The royal family had never coughed in her direction.

The third son of the king had certainly never spoken to her before.

"As two of a kind, it's past time we make ourselves known to each other," he said in a voice that was velvet. "Don't you think?"

In that moment, the smoke starting to seep inside the barn didn't matter. The mage hunters outside with their red banners and uniforms didn't matter.

Her voice was raw from smoke and screams, but she didn't care. "You have it, too. *Silverblood*."

He must have seen her use it that night.

Perhaps in response to the word, the foundation of the building around them shivered. Tracker's head whipped back in Everin's direction, and she could see the white of his teeth as he made a noise that sounded like she'd hurt him.

She'd never said the word before. Maybe it was true; maybe just saying the name of what she was would call on calamity itself.

Prince Alaric had stepped fully into the stall. His hands flew across Tracker's back, first as he positioned the riding blanket over his back and then as he affixed the saddle to him.

"What's going on?" It was all that Everin could think to say.

She'd risen fully to her feet, but beyond that, she hadn't the slightest idea what she should be doing. She'd entered the stables to evacuate the horses before the fire spread to their stables. There's been no *after*.

There'd certainly been no *this*.

Prince Alaric is a Silverblood.

Maybe if she told herself the words enough, she'd start to believe them.

"What's going on is we're leaving before they burn us alive."

"Your Majesty—" The words spluttered from her when she realized she hadn't been addressing him properly this entire time. "You don't need to do this. I'm sure the king could work with the guild on your behalf."

For the past twenty years, King Nikhil and Queen Roen had become the most powerful rulers on the continent. If anyone could bargain for a Silverblood's freedom, it would be the king and queen who had joined two kingdoms with their marriage.

The prince's amber-gold eyes were elsewhere. His hands were still busy with saddling Tracker as he said the words.

"They're dead. All of them."

Her mouth tasted of ash.

The Guild of Magic Study wasn't supposed to interfere with royal affairs, just as the royal family had always agreed to leave the guild to what it did best—study Silverblood and capture those with it in their veins before they destroyed too much with it.

It wasn't supposed to be like this.

A new thought occurred to her, and her heart lodged in her throat. "They knew to come here because there's two of us."

It was the ugly answer.

The only reason that Everin or the prince hadn't been able to go on with their lives, hiding the part of them which made them so dangerous to innocent people around them, was the fact that they had both been here. The silver substance which roamed within them—the thing that the guild called magic—was more detectable when more of it was concentrated in one place.

And the mage hunters' instruments never lied.

Even after she'd woken that morning months ago in a pool of silver liquid, she'd chosen to remain living her life as a kitchen hand. Instead of fleeing to the farthest, most blurred corner of any map she could get her hands on, she'd wanted to remain the same. She'd wanted to keep the life she'd fought so hard to have.

The royal family had been massacred because of her foolish thinking.

"They tried to protect you." Everin didn't know why she was still talking. She certainly wasn't making him feel any better, she was sure.

Prince Alaric's eyes flashed in the dim light. "I'm leaving the castle. I'm leaving it all. They won't stop."

He'd mounted Tracker and extended a hand to her. Ash had fallen on him and colored his black hair gray in spots, but it was still the darkest shade of black she'd ever seen. None of the boys she had once eyed even compared to him.

Everin backed away, and she felt his golden eyes tracking her.

She would run—run until her feet cracked and bled. She couldn't lead the mage hunters to the last remaining member of the royal family. She couldn't leave with the prince and think like this anymore.

Like she belonged with other people.

Silverblood or not, she would always hurt them.

"I can't—"

Prince Alaric pulled the edge of something worn and frayed from the interior of his black coat.

Even though she couldn't read the writing plainly on the spine, she knew what it was. It was something that was supposed to have been destroyed decades ago.

The part of her that wasn't her shuddered at the sight.

Even though she'd whispered, her words were too loud. "The Book of Dissimulation." Everin's knees almost gave.

This was the answer to their problem. The only answer—besides death.

The ancient text must have remained in the royal library all these years.

"It's missing pages. I need you if I'm going to find them." His molten eyes flicked to her face, and his eyebrows rose at what he must have seen there. "Unless you've made arrangements to some other prince behind my back already."

Her breath flew from her. "I'll have to tell him as we pass by."

When he helped swing her to Tracker's back, Everin found that she must have forgotten how to breathe.

The gods were toying with her. She must have perished on the stone floor of the kitchen. There was little other rational explanation.

When they rode for the forests beyond the castle, Everin was sure the trees parted for them.

CHAPTER TWO

The night was cold. But it wasn't the first time Everin had slept outside. Nor was it the first time she'd left behind a home.

It was, however, the first time she hadn't known what her future held.

Her eyes fell on their meager supplies left on the other side of the smoldering fire—and the bundle half-hidden from view. The key to any sort of future for them remained inside the pages of the ancient text that Alaric had saved from the castle's library.

The Book of Dissimulation.

Everin watched as the embers' glow flashed and faded to black coals. Enough heat radiated from it to reach her face and body, but she couldn't control the shiver that ran through her.

She wished that Tracker hadn't left earlier to wander the field north of them for nutrient-rich grass.

"Are you cold?"

Everin's heart jumped into her throat. Prince Alaric was standing above her, wearing only a thin shirt clinging to his chest and a pair of trousers. Underneath his shirt, she could see the shape of his defined shoulders and chest. She'd never seen him out of the black and gold trim coat that marked him a member of the royal family.

Everin moved her eyes to his face when she realized she'd been staring too long at places she shouldn't. "I'm fine."

But she felt that he hadn't missed the glance.

In the shadows of the trees near them, she thought she saw a glimmer in his gold eyes.

"Is that so?" he mused above her. "I wasn't aware that *fine* meant freezing."

Everin's mouth opened to object in the same moment that the son of a king crouched to the ground and slipped under the quilt that smelled of horses to lay beside her.

"What are you doing?" Blood rushed to Everin's face. She rolled out from under the quilt on the lightly frosted earth. Her chest was heaving where emotions she didn't care to name tangled inside her.

At once, the cold assaulted her, biting at her extremities. She didn't appreciate how both the cold and the prince had teamed up against her.

Alaric's eyebrows rose. "I can promise you, I'm as chaste as a priest."

She sat up, tucking her legs close. Everin's arms crossed against her chest.

She squinted at the prince who had stolen her quilt. "Why do I have the feeling that's a lie?"

"I *can* be chaste as a priest," Alaric amended. "Unless you want something else of me."

If there was any part of Everin's face that wasn't red, that wasn't the case any longer.

He's too distracting.

She fought to conceal the shivers as she said through her teeth, "That's not what I meant."

"What, pray tell, *did* you mean?"

Everin focused on the speckles of stars above them. It proved a challenge to look at him and make her point at the same time. "I don't want to hurt you."

"What ever are you talking about?"

"What's inside of me can hurt people. Even before I was—" Her throat lodged with words that wouldn't be spoken. Everin started again, "I don't want to hurt you."

He was silent so long that she was forced to meet his gaze again.

His face revealed no emotion as he asked, "Do you think you can hurt me just by sleeping beside me?"

Everin couldn't reply. She was too sure the answer was yes.

The prince continued in her silence, "We both carry it in our veins. This is the risk we both pose. To each other and from each other."

"Everin." The way he spoke her name was like how autumn winds beckoned to winter.

Something shifted in his face. "Few could ever hope to experience the sort of power that lives in your veins. Revel in it—or toil under the persecution of others for the very same cause. The choice is yours."

Her throat felt hoarse. What did she choose?

"How did you find out what you were?" she asked.

She wasn't sure if she asked it because she didn't know what else to say to his words or because she couldn't picture it. But in that moment, she needed to know.

A devilish smirk twitched to his lips. "Stop freezing yourself, and I'll tell you."

Everin's arms across her chest were rigid as stone as she crossed the distance that she'd put between them.

"As you wish, *my sire*." If this was the game he wished to play, then so be it.

As soon as she lifted the edge of the quilt to scoot under it, her body relaxed into the warmth against her will. His arm nearest her almost felt feverish in comparison to her cold skin.

Everin jerked her arm from where they'd been touching. This was a *prince*. Princes didn't sleep next to the girls who washed their dishes in the kitchens.

Even so, neither of them moved beyond that.

Up close, his gaze was even more sharp. She couldn't hide when he stared at her like that.

Her eyes moved elsewhere even as the sarcasm formed on her tongue. "Is this to your standards, my prince?"

But she had to peek to his face to see his reaction. She swallowed at what she saw. "Very."

He knows how to distract. Too well.

She'd asked him a question and deserved an answer, prince or no. "Tell me, then." She said, "How did you find out that you were—"

Everin stopped. She couldn't say the word again. She wouldn't risk it.

The prince's eyes moved to the shadows draping across their clearing. "It was ... my mother who realized."

"She must have been trying to protect you from it," Everin guessed. From what she remembered of Queen Roen, she had been a just and fair ruler and loving mother. She was sure the queen would have wanted her youngest child safe from the Guild. Even if that meant risking the wrath of their hunters if they ever found out what he was.

When he didn't say anything, she realized. The wounds must have been too fresh.

The misstep pained her, and she struggled to find what to say that wasn't about his recently slaughtered family.

"It happened for me when I woke one morning in ... the silver." It was the most she was willing to say of the name. She continued, "I always thought something like that was *caused* by something. But it's not."

"What does it feel like?" His eyes were hungry on her.

Everin's lips parted, and her eyebrows came together. "You ... don't know?"

"It's not strong for me yet."

Oh, right.

Everin knew only her own experience with it and the whispers and curses she'd heard among the kitchen hands and the others who had slept in alleys.

One of the few things she'd known about Silverblood beforehand was that the longer it was allowed to exist in a person, the stronger its power grew.

And the greater the danger.

It was why the Guild stole them away and executed the ones that ran.

"I acted as if I'd imagined it. But it can't be ignored." Everin's voice was a whisper. "It rests inside you like a snake, sleeping, until you let it snap. And when you do ... it gets fatter. Like a mouse bloating a snake's belly, it grows inside you."

Everin wasn't sure what possessed her to keep talking, but she couldn't stop herself. "The first time—the only time, really—was shortly after that. It *wanted* to be used. I didn't know what was going to happen, of course. I just—I was so angry that night. The coins I'd hidden were gone and—"

She took a breath. If she was going to say it, she needed to say it.

"It was the pond beyond the castle gardens. The one beyond the trees." She saw it as if it were before her now. It had been a natural pond, unlike the fountains and shallow pools of water that surrounded the castle which had been dug by the gardeners.

"One moment, it was as it should have been. And the next—it was as if it were mid-winter, and the surface had frozen over in thick ice. But it wasn't ice." Everin paused. "I remember that it turned silver. And it never turned back. The water solidified to … something else. I spent the rest of the night and the next day concealing it with bushes and grass."

"I saw you," he admitted. "Or at least, what you left behind."

A lump formed in her throat. She'd guessed as much when he knew who she was in the horses' stalls.

That night was when she'd known. Silverblood couldn't be ignored.

But maybe it could be suppressed. Her eyes moved to the bundle across from them, only dimly illuminated by the dying coals. The faded lettering on its side were like foreign runes to her eyes.

"That's really it, isn't it? And the Guild has suggested that they had it all this time."

When she tried to meet his gaze, the golden eyes that marked him unmistakably as the king's son moved to the book.

Instead of answering her question, he asked, "What do you know of this book?"

"The Book of Dissimulation?" In truth, she'd thought it was another rumor—like Silverblood.

How wrong she'd been.

Everin remembered back to those rumors, the tales traded by the other kitchen hands about exactly what treasures the royal family must have been hiding in that gilded library of theirs.

"It can hide who we are. The power," Everin said. "It's supposed to stifle it—and maybe more."

"It tells of a ritual invoking magic." Prince Alaric's eyes stared through hers as he spoke. "Even without those missing pages, it's clear that's what where this is heading."

"Is that all? What else is in it?" she asked.

She couldn't see his face as he stared forward. "It was considered mere rumor for many years. I almost didn't believe it existed myself until I discovered it by chance, hidden in my family's library. It's a book of how to survive as one of us, in some ways. But also ... of power. It's why the Guild has wanted it so badly."

"Why were pages torn from it in the first place?" she wondered.

His thumb pressed against the side of the pages as if in reverence. There was a look to his golden eyes that faded too fast for her to catch it.

"The pages detailed a forbidden ritual," he said simply.

Forbidden? Everin blinked.

Well, it makes sense, she figured after a moment. *The Guild would want to forbid anything that keeps them from carrying out their service of controlling Silverbloods.*

She remembered he'd been studying the text ever since they'd left the castle. She'd even leafed through the book herself, even though she couldn't read.

Even so, the thought of a magical ritual was enough to curdle the contents of her stomach. She'd had enough of anything so-called *magical* for a lifetime.

Would you rather be hunted for your Silverblood for the remainder of your life? And be a danger to yourself and anyone around you?

Her eyes fell on the prince, and she knew the answer.

It was a feat to pull her chin up and appear resolute from under a horse's quilt, but she thought she managed it. "Fine," she said.

"If we're going to go through with this, Everin," Prince Alaric said, and she watched the way his mouth said her name with an odd fascination, "promise me something. But only if you'll mean it."

She swallowed. "What is it?"

"What's inside that book—what we're going to do—will be permanent. Promise me that you want this. That whatever future awaits us on the other side of these pages is one that you want."

Everin only hesitated a moment.

It was all it took her to remember that without this chance to suppress the part of her that grew like a snake trapped in a too-tight glass cage, the glass cage would burst.

"I promise."

CHAPTER THREE

"**A**re you sure you're ready for this?"

Alaric's breath brushed against her cheek as he whispered against her ear.

They were dressed in cloaks that hid their faces as they moved with the crowds walking from the markets and into the greater city. Even so, Everin felt much too exposed.

She knew their time was running short for finding the missing pages of the book—they couldn't run from the mage hunters forever like this—and they'd already spotted some of their red cloaks in the sprawling city.

After what had happened at the castle, their presence in every city was to be expected. And Alaric had reassured her that relatively few mage hunters actually carried Silverblood-detecting instruments.

It didn't make her feel much better. But when his hand found hers to lead them through the crowd, something in her chest jumped and gave her a little more courage.

Not long after, they found the front of the building that Alaric had indicated on his map. Its front was dark, and she could see that the inside was too, well-separated as it was from the bustle of the streets.

She felt Alaric watching her.

"Do you want to go back?"

But she kept seeing the red flare of their cloaks in the crowd. The city was crawling with them. If they came back another day, they risked the chance of one of them having a detection instrument.

Which would guarantee their being found.

Everin shook her head. The piece of paper was folded in her tight fist. She could do this small thing for them, at least.

Yet, as she walked through the doors to the city's library inside, she realized just how out of her depth she was. Shelves upon shelves of books closed around her, more than she'd ever seen in her life. Their spines stared back at her, mocking her.

Though the library was mostly empty, a few patrons hovered at desks and along the racks. Most of them wore a pin with the symbol for the city's academy on their fine tailored coats. Their shoes *clacked* softly against the tiled floor whereas her boots squeaked. She and Alaric had trudged through mud to escape the mage hunters, and she'd scrubbed and soaked her shoes as best as she could just earlier in the day.

They were dry on the outside, or so she'd thought.

Everin ignored them, the patrons and books both, and walked straight for the central desk of the library. Scarce light slipped through the high windows of the building—it seemed as if the books didn't like the sun.

She wished that she could've had Alaric by her side. She felt she stuck out like a sore thumb.

He would be at home here.

But she knew that would have meant they'd be recognized easier. His eyes were an unmistakable shade. It was a danger just to have him next to her in the city.

The librarian met Everin's greetings with barely a murmur, only looking up from what he was doing when she held out the note for him. As he read its contents, his eyes narrowed at it from behind his glasses and his mouth twitched.

Finally, he looked at her straight-on. "Not from the academy, then. You know the rarity of such a thing?" Before she could answer, he said, "No, of course I don't have this."

Everin tried not to let the disappointment overcome her, but it was difficult. They'd sacrificed and risked so much, all for a condescending refusal.

"You couldn't … check? Maybe there's something here that points to where they would be?" Everin heard herself ask, but her cheeks were already warmed through from the letdown and a quiet, funny kind of anger.

She should be leaving now. Her squeaky boots wanted to turn around and go.

But the librarian was looking at her now differently than he had before. He'd already replaced the note in her hands, though he looked like he wanted it back.

Suddenly, he swept away from her. Before he disappeared past a heavy wood door, he murmured, "Stay there. I'll check."

Everin supported herself against the counter, trying not to notice if any of the academy students were looking at her. It was nearly empty, anyway, and she imagined most of the city would have rather crawled the markets on a day like today than waste into dust inside this tomb of a building.

He'd left his glasses resting on his desk, and Everin briefly picked them up to see how the skinny blades of light passed through them.

It was then that she noticed something behind the librarian's desk.

She felt like she was being held underwater, like a great pressure pinched her chest of air.

There, pinned to a wooden community notice board hanging on the wall was a sketch of her likeness. It held a bare resemblance to her, as if the one doing the sketching had seen her from across a crowd, but it was plainly her. Her auburn hair was highlighted against her too-red cheeks and brown eyes. She stared forward at the sketch-her who stared back at her.

With her face under a cloak or in a crowd, someone might not notice they were one and the same. Up close, however ...

Everin turned, failing to keep her boots from squeaking as she vacillated between running and walking to the door she'd arrived from. In her head, she imagined the words that might be written underneath the sketch of her face.

Wanted for murder.

High treason.

Silverblood.

It didn't matter exactly what they said. What mattered was the face above them.

As the door thudded shut behind her, she considered just how much of a fool she'd been, thinking she could try to walk this freely among people after what had happened at the castle.

And considering what ran through her veins, maybe she shouldn't.

The screams of humans and animals came to her again, overlapping with the constant stream of conversations from the street walkers carried by the southerly wind. Everin's heartrate raced too fast, and sweat pressed strands of her hair against her face. She felt she might be sick.

"What's wrong?" Alaric's eyes missed nothing, and he was beside her in an instant from where he'd concealed himself in the shade of the building. He steadied her and pushed hair out of her face.

"Fliers. They had fliers inside," she managed to say. "We need to go." She pushed herself forward at the expense of her balance and tried to start for the street, but he stopped her.

Alaric searched her expression. "Slow down. It's okay. Breathe," he said, pulling her instead to the alley where he'd been.

Everin tried to do as he'd commanded, but she knew they needed to leave. Now.

Breathing could come later.

"We need to go. The librarian—I think he knew," she gasped.

"Look into my face, Everin. Look." He held her steady against the brick wall, forcing her gaze into his. "Do this for me now. Trust me."

After several seconds, her eyes stopped bouncing from one point to the next and settled on him. His breaths were a welcome breeze, brushing strands of hair from her face. The molten gold of his eyes dominated her vision, and she found, even in the shade of the alley, specks of darker and lighter points within it.

"You're safe. You can breathe here," he murmured, holding her eyes on him.

"How can you say that?" Everin whispered. "He's going to tell them what I am."

The *what* had slipped out instead of *who*. Because, no matter her innocence of what they'd thought she'd done, she was certainly guilty of being a Silverblood.

When it came to that, there was no misunderstanding.

"Their headquarters is far," he said. "The best this librarian could do is try to contact the hunters stationed here. We have time to escape the city, but we need to blend in first."

But his unwavering gaze on her wasn't doing much to keep her heartrate down. She tried to breathe anyway and nodded, not trusting her voice.

"First though," he said, his voice still low, "I need to know something, Everin. Don't speak, just nod. Do you think you can do that for me?"

She nodded again. Her heart fluttered despite her attempts to control it.

"What were on the papers? You? Me?"

Everin collected enough air to respond, "A sketch of me."

She felt his eyes on her, watching her as he held her arms steady with his. "And ... what did they say?"

But all Everin could do was shake her head. A spike of blood rushed to her cheeks. She was illiterate.

This was the difference between them, as it always had been. He'd been raised to study cultures, literature, war strategy, history, fine arts.

She'd been raised to survive.

"I'm sorry," Alaric whispered softly. "That was thick of me. I didn't mean to upset you more." He closed his eyes as he seemed to think. "I should have done this instead of you. I risked them finding you."

"They would have recognized you at once," she breathed.

His eyes were bright when he opened them again.

"And yet, I'm not the only one of us with such distinct features." His smirk made the tips of her ears redden.

"I don't know what you're talking about," she said as she crossed her arms. But as she did, a strand of her warm auburn hair moved across her face.

"Really?" He tucked the lock back behind one of her ears before she could. "I find that hard to believe."

She looked at him accusingly. This had all been part of his plan.

Without realizing it, she'd regained her breath where she'd lost it before. Though his comments did nothing for her heartrate.

His expression changed to something like intrigue. "Or perhaps you just want me to say it."

"Say it?"

"To admit—" he started.

A commotion on the streets outside their alley cut him off. The constant hum of conversation and industry had broken off for raised voices.

Instead of speaking, they ran farther inside the alley. While Everin had never lived within these city walls, she knew enough about living on the streets to know that alleys, though sometimes filled with less than friendly folk, were never populated by city guards or Guild hunters.

It was a place to get lost. A place where Everin felt comfortable, away from the eyes of students, librarians, mage hunters, street vendors, and passerby all.

But their shortcut didn't last forever. Alaric stopped them as he glanced into the street where their passageway ended.

Even from her hidden position within the alley, the city gates had risen into view. They were close.

Maybe fifteen minutes, and they'd be on the other side of them.

There was something to Alaric's expression, however, that made her pause. Careful to keep her hood raised, she joined him at the edge of the street.

Her eyebrows came together. The streets had clogged before the gates, and the longer she looked, the worse things got.

"They've blockaded the gates out of the city," Alaric said under his breath. His jaw was tight as he whispered a curse.

But that wasn't all. It appeared they had partitioned a section of the crowd to one side.

"They're separating the girls ... the ones that look anything like me," she breathed.

Everin turned to look back along the passage they'd cut through. It led no other way except back to the library where she'd been potentially identified.

"This is my fault. I shouldn't have ... maybe if I hadn't have spoken so much to him—"

"Everin, no." Alaric was next to her at once. "This is my fault for bringing us to a large city so soon. I was an idiot, thinking they would be looking at places closer to the castle for us. I should have rushed us out of this city as soon as you left that place."

"No," she said, "I needed that. I would have given us away with how nervous I was." In a smaller voice, she added, "Thank you. I don't know how we'll get past the hunters and out of this city, but I vow we will."

But Alaric was looking at something sticking out of her dress pocket. She followed his gaze.

His smirk made her heart beat too loudly.

"And we'll do it because of you, sticky fingers." Lightly, too lightly, he traced the red that had appeared at the tip of her ear.

She hadn't truly meant to pocket them.

Before she could say anything in her defense, his eyes shifted to her face. "How well can you act?"

CHAPTER FOUR

As Everin moved through the line out of the city, the sun dragged itself across the sky. They were running short of time. Alaric had informed her that, when the mage hunters were on alert like this, it was protocol for them to lock the gates at sundown.

According to her math, they had less than an hour.

The women and girls around her had seemed to realize this as well, and the general conversation had turned from mild annoyance and even intrigue about the Silverblood on the run to a cold desperation.

Everin looked to the other line, the one in which Alaric had been sorted into with the rest of the men. His absence rattled her nerves, and she reminded herself of his words to her before they'd been split up.

"Stay alive. No matter what you need to do, get back to me."

She'd promised him, and she wasn't about to break her word.

And, somehow, it appeared their disguises might actually work. Alaric was wearing the thick glasses she'd taken from the librarian to better hide his unusual eyes, and they'd found chimney soot to muddle the reds of her hair closer to a brown-black. The smell of doused fire clung to her like a ghost.

Everin had wrapped most of her hair in a cloth about her head, and more cloth was wrapped around her body under her dress to hide the knife she kept on her for defense. Alaric carried the rest of the few supplies they'd dared to bring with them, which fortunately excluded the book.

However, the closer she got to those inspecting them, the more foolish and transparent her disguise felt. Her heart rattled in her cage. Alaric was standing on the other side of the gates, and his eyes met hers.

He'd gotten through.

It was then that a voice commanded, "Her. Bring her over here."

He was a large man, almost like two put together. The red of his coat burned into her vision. He was one of them.

Her heart skipped a beat. They'd found her.

It was time to run and damn the consequences.

But it wasn't her that the giant of a man had grabbed by the wrist. A girl with reddish-brown hair much like her own was pulled from the line behind her.

"I've done nothing wrong," she said through gritted teeth. "Let me go!"

"Stop struggling. We only want to ask a question or two."

It was the last she heard of their conversation before the rumble of the voices around her drowned them out. She could feel in the girls and women around her how they looked away at this part. They didn't want to see or know what would come next.

They were released again. The guards were letting most everyone through now. Chatter of what the day's market-crawling had brought them and treats to be eaten on the road filled the air.

Pickled sweet onion. Salted pork sticks. Glazed pastries. Dark cherries.

For a moment, Everin thought of her ma.

It was then that she noticed furtive movement in the shadow of the city gates, away from the crowds and lines.

It was there they'd dragged the girl. But now, instead of one hunter by her side, there were three. One of them had hit her, and she had doubled over in pain.

It's not her. She's not the one guilty of being a Silverblood.

But no one else had seen the open assault, or if they had, they refused to see it anymore.

Everin couldn't look away. All they had to do was test her blood to see the red of it. A few drops, and she'd be cleared. But they weren't doing that.

They're bored, she thought. *They don't care if she's not the one.*

And then, another possibility: *Maybe she's one, too.*

But they'd taken her to be Everin. No matter what, this girl didn't deserve that.

First the castle staff. The horses. Then Alaric's family.
Now this girl.

How many more would pay for what she'd turned into? She was beginning to lose count.

Cold sweat beaded along the back of her neck. She was free. She was out. All she had to do now was follow the overwhelming flow of the crowd and meet Alaric on this side of the gates.

The image of the girl wouldn't leave her, standing before her like a phantom.

"Everin. You're okay. I thought—" Alaric cut himself off. "It doesn't matter. We're out now."

He'd found her in the swarm of travelers outside the gates. The sun's long rays colored his face a honey tone.

Everin couldn't seem to move her feet or feel the relief that Alaric was. It must have been plain on her face because Alaric stopped suddenly.

"What's wrong?" he asked.

Her voice was a whisper. "They took someone else."

Alaric was quiet. She could hear what went unsaid in his silence.

"It's us or this person."

If they intervened or tried to stop what was going on with the mage hunters, then they'd undoubtedly be discovered themselves. At a glance, they passed for different people than what was likely on their wanted posters.

But Everin held no illusions about how easily they'd be identified if they came face-to-face with those hunting them.

It was irrational to think she could save the girl who'd been mistaken for her. Everin told herself this as they moved with the shuffle of people on the other side of the city gates. They weren't the villains here. No, that title belonged to the mage hunters.

They had no part in their heinous acts.

What if someone had done this for me? Intervened?

Alaric did, she thought. *Without him, I would have been carried off in chains like a dog.*

Tears prickled at her eyes. She saw the slap in her mind. Felt the sting of the hit against her skin.

But there would be worse to come for the girl.

The sun was touching the horizon now. It would be dark soon, and the gates would close.

"I'm going back," she said under her breath.

Alaric froze next to her. His voice was equally low. "I can't let them take you."

Something in her chest fluttered at his words. She reminded herself that he just meant that they were in this together. That they needed each other in order to find the lost pages of the book.

"Then we make sure that doesn't happen," she said, holding his golden gaze. Her heart was beating too fast. "We create a distraction. Something to give her the chance to get away if she's really ..."

One of us, Everin thought but didn't say. Even here, in their whispers, it felt too risky to imply.

"I'm going back," she repeated to him. Nothing would stop her.

He closed his eyes for a moment. He opened them a moment later before taking her by the hand away from the river of people pouring from the city.

"You have to make sure they don't see you," he whispered in her ear. "I can keep the doors open a little longer. But not for long. If they're going to catch you, run."

He slipped something from their pack to her pocket.

"What is this?" She ran her fingers over the object. It felt like it was paper wrapped into a small tube.

"Just a little something the hunters raiding the castle left behind," he explained with a devilish smile.

***

Everin pushed herself into the crowd fighting to get inside the city as the sun set. Behind her, two donkeys were suddenly cut loose from their cart. One raced past the line of people waiting to get outside, and the other stood, braying and tail twitching as it backed away from those that ran to contain it.

Silently, she thanked Alaric and stopped looking for him in the sea of faces. They would find each other on the other side again.

Though only minutes had passed since she'd seen the girl and the mage hunters, there was no sign left of them. They were gone from the shadows of the gates.

Her stomach churned as she considered how foolish this whole idea had been.

Either she'd already been let go from the mage hunters or they'd discovered she was a Silverblood by now and had secured her from escape.

It was a stupid idea. She couldn't even save herself against these people. How could she save someone else?

She was going to get her and Alaric locked inside the city where the mage hunters had all night to find them. Her hands shook as she considered her foolishness. The evening's shadows had grown and massed over the city.

Out of the periphery of her vision, Everin saw a flash of red. The mage hunters were crowding around a figure, and she could barely make out the girl being led away in chains. Bruises had bloomed along her jaw. Everin's stomach clenched at the sight.

It was now or never.

Everin pinched a bead of Silverblood from the prick she'd made on her finger and touched it to the end of the object's wick. As soon as she did, the end started to produce smoke where her blood seeped through the string. She dropped it as the crowd crushed her back.

She knew the instant that the Silverblood had bled through the wick to the middle of it. A trail of smoke morphed into a mass like a dark raincloud pregnant with thunder. Those in a radius of several feet were engulfed in the thick smoke, and the crowd started to panic around her.

Her pulse raced as she kept her feet straight and her eyes on the spot along the wall she'd seen before setting off the smoke bomb. But Everin hadn't bargained on the curdled scream on the air she heard then.

"Silverblood!"

Her cut ached at the word like the cursed substance in her veins was responding to it. Several people pushed against Everin, sending her to the ground.

Her skin scraped against stone where she fell. Around her, the crowd pushed dangerously out of control. Whether or not others had discovered there was a Silverblood in their midst remained to be seen, but the accusation was enough to cause a panicked frenzy.

I'll be trampled if I don't move.

Everin scraped her skin further as she lurched from the thick of it. As she scrambled from the chaos, she realized she had a vantage point she hadn't before.

At this height, she could see through the smoke. The sight across the street from her made her pulse pound harder.

Everin got to her feet and ran in the direction of the girl bundled on the ground. Her back was pressed against the wall, and her eyes were wide as Everin approached. She was in shock.

At first, she jerked away from her.

Everin crouched low. "I'm not one of them. I promise. But we have to go. The gates are closing for good soon."

She tried to press her hand against the girl's, but she slipped farther away from her. She stared at Everin with wide brown eyes that were not unlike her own.

This could have been me.

"Please," Everin said in rough whispers. "I don't want to see them hurt anyone else. Please come with me."

Everin held out her hand to the girl. Behind them, she could hear the city guards corral the crowds into civility again. Their chance was passing.

The other girl took her hand, and before the smoke dissipated entirely, they ran through it like wraiths in the dying light.

CHAPTER FIVE

Everin's coughs came hard enough to draw tears to her eyes. She and the girl the mage hunters had accosted were on the other side of the city gates. Night had fallen on the land.

When she seemed to regain her speech, the girl turned to her and said, "Thank you. Thank you so much."

Her red-brown hair was loosened in strands from the braid it had been in. She appeared to be on the verge of tears but aggressively wiped the back of her eyes before they had appeared as if willing them back.

"I was afraid they were going to take me," she continued.

Everin's heart sped up. *Is she ...?*

Is she a Silverblood, too?

"It's okay," Everin said. "I'm just glad we got out." But even as she spoke to try to soothe her, her eyes were on the dissipating crowd around them.

Alaric still hadn't met up with them. Where was he?

"They wouldn't listen to me. I told them I wasn't evil," the girl continued. "But they wouldn't listen." Her eyes darted back to Everin's face. "What will happen when they see I'm gone? What if they come after me?"

"We'll leave here together," Everin said, her eyes still on the thinning mass of people. "Just as soon as I find our other companion."

Her stomach churned with a new fear. What if Alaric hadn't gotten out?

Had she just traded saving one person from the mage hunters for giving up another?

But the girl didn't seem placated by her words. A strange silence had drifted between them. Everin looked up, ready to assure her that they would be free of the Guild's hunters, even if Everin had to come back here herself, when she saw something else was wrong.

She was staring at the punctured skin on one of her hands. Or rather, the bead of silver that had started dripping from the spot. It was where she'd pricked herself to activate the smoke bomb.

"You're one of them." She heard the girl say the words. "You're the girl they're searching for."

A gulf had widened where Everin's heart was. She couldn't respond, though the girl kept talking.

"The monster that killed them all," the girl that was her mirror continued.

"I didn't do that." Everin's voice was hoarse when she spoke. "I didn't hurt them."

But the girl she'd saved was backing away, fear and something else in her eyes.

A moment later, she realized it was disgust.

"Of course it was you," the girl said, her eyes still locked on the Silverblood Everin bled. "How could it not be when you have poison inside?"

Everin had nothing to say to that. She hadn't realized she had stepped towards her until the girl jerked back from her.

She turned and left Everin in the dark.

As the minutes passed, Everin knew she should have been moving by now. She was probably reporting her to the same magic hunters who had terrorized her before.

She wouldn't. They were going to hurt her.

But an ugly feeling rose inside her that said otherwise.

Shadows wrapped themselves around the trees and the city gates she'd just escaped. How many more towns were there to be like this? How long could they last, narrowly avoiding the Guild?

Everin wanted desperately to restore her life back to what it had been a week ago. She imagined her life like a spinning coin on a table. If only she could catch it and spin it the other way again.

Back to who she'd been.

A cloaked figure had started for her in the dim quiet of the dispersed crowds. Everin's hand went to her hidden knife before she saw the gold of his eyes and the quick quirk of his smile.

He must have seen her expression a second later when he pulled her closer to him to walk together, hand in hand.

Everin almost recoiled from him before she could stop herself.

"Chaste as a priest, remember?" His smile left his face. Under his breath, he asked, "What happened? Where is she?"

Everin just shook her head.

"We're being watched. I suspect ..." Alaric started.

He didn't have to finish. They had to appear calm, like they had normal lives just like the rest of the folk agitated by the little scrap of excitement that had ended their trip to the city and markets.

I suspect she went back to them, was what he probably meant to say, but Everin didn't want to accept that.

It would have meant accepting that Everin had put them both in more danger by trying to play hero. And accepting that turning in a monster was more important to the girl than maybe even her safety.

The latter thought disturbed Everin. It would have meant the girl thought Everin more of a threat than the mage hunters who had arrested her on the slightest of suspicions and even hurt her.

Is the silver inside me so dangerous?

But, of course, she knew the answer to that.

Everin pinched the end of her finger to stem the bleeding, but the smell of it was getting to her head.

Even after they safely located Tracker and left behind the bustling city, she couldn't stop thinking about the girl throughout the night and into the following day.

"Everin. You're not talking."

Alaric's voice made her jump.

They'd stopped riding only when night slipped into an early dawn. She supposed she hadn't fooled Alaric into thinking she'd slept that entire time, after all.

"What's wrong?" he continued, watching her from across the low fire he'd built.

She shook her head at the smolders. "Nothing. I'm fine."

But his gaze was piercing. "Don't lie. At least not to me."

Suddenly, he rose and sat next to her. "If we don't have this ... Someone left to talk to ... You see where I'm going with this."

"I do," Everin admitted. She rubbed her eyes like that would make the images behind them go away.

If they didn't have this, the companionship of one another, then they had nothing. Most all of Alaric's family had been murdered. And she'd long been on her own.

"I'm sorry. It's just ..." Everin stopped, and her fists curled together. "Why are they doing this? Why did they have to kill so many innocent people?"

"I don't know, Everin." His voice sounded strange and unlike him.

Everin chastised herself. *He's thinking of them, I'm sure.*

His eldest brother, the heir to the throne. And his parents.

Everin's fists loosened. "Maybe if ... I turned myself in, this would stop. The innocents dying and being hurt."

And maybe ... I deserve it.

Alaric jerked upright. "I never want to hear you say that." He moved one hand against her face to angle her eyes back to his. There was no looking away, though her cheeks rushed with heat.

"Everin." She resisted a shudder at how he said her name. "You must resist them at all costs. Do you understand?"

She found herself short of breath, but she managed a nod.

What the Guild did with the Silverbloods they captured ... Well, they were only rumors, as no one could enter one of their towers without first swearing loyalty to the Guild, but they weren't pretty rumors.

Even so, she didn't relish the idea of finding out.

"Why are the people allowing this? The Guild murdered the royal family." Everin's hands rushed through her hair. There should have been riots in the streets, not markets and street vendors shouting out their concoctions. "It shouldn't be like this. The two are supposed to be separate."

Alaric stared into the fire. "The Guild has always been envious of the power the crown wields. They want total control. So ... When their detectors found a trace of silver at the castle, they were all too eager to slit the throats of my family. And then they blamed us, Silverbloods, for it. The most convenient scapegoat is one that already acts guilty."

His expression was hollow, and she could see the smolders of the low fire burst in the deep black of his irises where it reflected back.

There didn't seem to be words enough for such a thing, so she let the fire's crackling be the only noise between them.

What Alaric had said certainly made sense, but the world still seemed too stable to her. Didn't anyone have qualms about the dynasty of golden kings coming to an end—or rather to a point where the only heir left was one with Silverblood?

It was then that she remembered something important he'd mentioned before. A small detail she'd overlooked.

Everin swallowed. To open the wound again or not? She shouldn't, she knew.

But it was bothering her more the longer she thought on it.

"That look is my favorite, perhaps." Prince Alaric's lips twitched up when she met his gaze.

Her eyes darted away. Was he enjoying this?

"What do you mean?"

"I can already read you like a book, do you know that?" His smile when he said it made something in her throat catch.

For some reason, she felt she wanted to be more mysterious to him. It was childish, she knew.

"What is it?" he continued. "I think I could die if I don't know what caused those lips to pout like that."

"*Pout*—" She started over. "I wasn't pouting. I was think-ing." She got to her feet. She was sure she shouldn't be speaking to a prince in this way.

Although she was less sure where she intended to go or really, why she'd risen in the first place.

"Everin. I'm sorry if I upset you. Please, sit." He gestured back to the blankets they'd made for their seats. "I want to ask you something."

"It's alright." After a breath, she took her seat near him again. "What did you want to know?"

His eyes flicked over to her face again. A slow smirk appeared on his lips. "Do I fluster you?"

Everin's eyebrows soared. This prince knew all her buttons and how to push them.

"Of course you do," she said at last.

"Why?"

Everin laughed. She couldn't help it. But as he was looking at her, she realized he truly expected an answer. As if it weren't obvious enough.

"Because you're ..." Everin waved her hand in the air, gestur-ing all around him. Finally, it came out. "Attractive."

And enigmatic. And frustrating. And baffling.

His eyes were dangerous. "And you're not?"

"And a royal," she pointed out, ignoring his remark. For some reason, it pained her to explain this. Didn't he realize the stark differences between them?

Prince Alaric captured and held her gaze. "But you're even more than that. Don't you realize?"

His hand moved and suddenly, he held hers. Carefully, he extended her finger where she'd pricked it to ignite the smoke bomb at the city gates.

"Do you know why our blood can spark chemicals such as those within their weapons?" he asked, the gold of his eyes visible just beyond his dark lashes. His fingers circled her joint.

She shook her head, not trusting in her voice.

"Don't you find it curious that our very presence makes them call us monsters? Those without power either envy or fear it. Sometimes, both." Alaric pressed his thumb to her finger where the pinprick had been, though the wound had dried by now. "It worked because, like fire, our blood is pure energy. Pure power."

He released her hand, and she stared at where silver had bled from her.

"Power," she echoed. "Then why does it feel like a poison? Like something that will infect me?"

Alaric was quiet for some time before saying, "I don't think it's an accident that it chose you."

Everin looked up suddenly. "What are you saying?"

"I think only the strong can handle it," he said. "In fact, I know it's true."

But Everin couldn't be so sure. She knew how to scrape by. How to shapeshift when she needed. How to become invisible so the guards didn't heckle her for living in the alleys. How to fit in with early morning and late night workers.

Those were her powers. That was how she was strong, if she could really call it that.

Not by this consuming poison.

After some silence, he cocked his head at her, his smile blazing across his face. "Do you really find me attractive?"

She could feel her face turn scarlet. Before she could stop it, her fool mouth blurted, "Of course I do. Look at you. Why do you ask?"

His smile was incessant. "No reason. At all."

Everin fell silent. She shouldn't be admitting this to a prince. His grin dropped.

"What's wrong?"

She shook her head. He wasn't going to understand, she was slowly realizing.

He wasn't some field boy across the way. And she wasn't the daughter of monarchy.

Before she could begin to explain, Everin remembered what she'd been about to ask him before he'd flustered her. She held up a finger.

"You got a question from me. So, I get one from you," she proposed.

Alaric's eyebrows twitched just for a moment.

"Oh, really? What did you want to know?"

Everin chewed on the thought. It seemed they were speaking more freely between them now, but this was another matter entirely.

"Well," she started, "you said they … killed your parents and brother." *Great start,* she thought to herself but didn't stop. "What about the other prince?"

The queen and king had had three heirs: Adrian, Aleksander, and Alaric.

Alaric's expression changed completely. All traces of emotion turned to a strange blankness. "He wasn't at the castle." He stared forward into the fire.

Everin regretted the change in topic at once. She should have dropped the matter there, she knew. But if they had help, it could make all the difference.

"Then it's possible he yet lives, Alaric. That the Guild hasn't gotten to him yet. Perhaps if you contact him—"

"He wouldn't understand." Alaric's voice was low. He stared at his palm. Something had scratched it, though it hadn't started to bleed the silver within. "He wouldn't accept it."

Alaric's open palm formed a fist.

"He would kill me on the spot."

CHAPTER SIX

Their peace lasted a week longer.

The nights under the broad expanse of stars with a prince had been entrancing. During the days, she traversed through book shops in every village, township, and city marked on the map that Prince Alaric had managed to save from what had once been his home.

After what had happened during their first venture into a city, the prince had stayed well away from each settlement to ensure their identities remained hidden. Or so they'd hoped.

They still hadn't found one of the missing pages, but something else had found them tonight.

As Everin bundled as many of their supplies as she could within her arms, she considered what had given them away.

Or rather, *who*.

As she mounted Tracker behind Prince Alaric, she heard the strange noises in the woods around them. Her front pressed into his black coat, and she was sure he could feel her heart hammer through the fabric of their clothes.

Though they hadn't seen them yet, there could be no doubt. The mage hunters were upon them.

Was it the librarian in Sarshae?

The din of their raised voices bounced against the surface of the tree trunks surrounding them. Everin's breathing quickened. Soon, they would be near enough to them for her to hear their words.

Perhaps it had been the bookseller in Riddarant. There had been many more curious objects in her store rather than books.

But another possibility occurred to her, almost too obvious to consider.

It was the girl who the mage hunters had taken to be me.

Everin bit down on her tongue, hard enough to make her gasp. She couldn't allow herself to fall apart just because their enemies had found them.

Until they found the last pages of the Book of Dissimulation, this was their life.

If they ever found them.

It was then she realized Tracker wasn't outpacing them.

Her words came out in a single breath as Tracker leapt over a fallen log. "How can we lose them?"

In her arms, his body was tense like a loaded crossbow. She was never as close to him as she was when they rode. It made her nervous, being this close to another person—least of all a prince.

Before Prince Alaric could answer her, a shout to their direct south soared through the trees to them.

"Surrender your prisoner!"

Her jaw slackened a degree. They thought her a *ransomer*?

He'd leaned into her when he spoke. "They're trying to trick us."

She'd heard tales of the mage hunters' cunning and ruthlessness. They were masters at getting what they wanted.

She heard another voice join in. "Release the prince or your life will be forfeit!"

"They would kill us both." Prince Alaric veered Tracker in a sharp turn away from the new voice.

She heard what went unsaid in his words. The names of his family that they'd already slain. King Nikhil, Queen Roen, and his eldest brother, Prince Adrian.

A bolt arced above their heads, causing leaves to spill over them as they glided over the ground. It was the kind of shot that was deliberate—a warning or a demonstration.

Everin's teeth clamped together. Their trickery wouldn't work with them, but their weapons might.

"You feel it even now, don't you? The pull of it?" She barely heard the prince's words over the shouting of their pursuers.

Breath caught in Everin's throat. "What are you saying?"

But she knew. The Silverblood in her had stirred like a snake, dancing. As if it would do what it wanted. As if it had *wants*.

She heard him curse. "It's not working for me. I'm not strong enough with it yet." Alaric's voice caught between gritted teeth. Between his words, she heard what he was asking.

Everin had never killed. In all the years she'd lived on the streets and when she had still been small enough to sleep in barrels, she had never brought herself that low.

Before she'd been hired as a kitchen hand, she'd lied and stolen her fill. But never killed.

She remembered her ma in her last days, the oversized sleeve draping her arm as she held it out for Everin. Her skin had been uncomfortably warm, but she hadn't been able to take her hand away.

She'd given her that sickness. Everin had recovered, and so she had assumed Ma would.

Her eyes flicked around her, seeing the woods again.

This is no time to fall apart, she told herself again. But she could feel reality slipping by her like a bad dream.

"Everin, they're going to kill us." For once, the bravado and charm were gone from Alaric's voice.

The change in Alaric scared her nearly most of all. Tracker narrowly jumped past a thick bramble, though he hadn't been quick enough to keep the bushes from scraping against them, and Everin felt the silver well from the cut.

Tracker's scream shot through the air as an arrow skimmed his flank, nearly piercing it through.

Everin didn't think. Thought had left her like roaches under a light.

She'd never purposefully called on it before, and she didn't now.

All she did was turn at her waist, her hands still locked around the prince's middle while she faced the direction behind them.

She'd thought it had started as a scream.

She wasn't sure what it had ended like.

The force of it propelled the three of them even farther than Tracker had jumped. Everin's head slammed against something too solid, and disorientation sliced through her.

***

In a blink, the forest was changed. She was silent as her eyes devoured the scene that stretched on and on—even farther than she could see.

The trees behind them had been reduced to stumps, smoke trails still lingering over some. The ones on the periphery that had survived had been cracked at their middle, and Everin was struck by how humanlike they seemed, as if they were bending down to pluck something.

The second thing she noticed was the gray. It was everywhere. In a panic, she looked to the skies for proof that her color sight hadn't been stolen as a price for calling on that part of her. But even the heavens seemed more charcoal than black.

Alaric's voice pierced the silence. "It's the Silverblood."

The world seemed to shiver at the word.

She didn't even realize she had been trembling. She didn't remember when Alaric had slipped off Tracker either. His forehead pressed to hers, and a sea of gold engulfed her vision.

Everin couldn't speak.

As best as they could estimate, the destruction stretched well on for a mile, but they stopped before they could find the outer boundary of the site. When they found signs of their pursuers' bodies, her knees pressed against the ground that she'd made barren as she heaved.

Her stomach still roiled as she wiped the back of her hand against her mouth, but she needed it to stop. His touch was light as he moved her hair out of the way.

"Let's go. You shouldn't see this," he murmured beside her.

"No." The word was barely more than a whisper, but she forced it out. "I need to know how many."

She wasn't sure why it mattered so much. But it did.

She had to know how many lives she'd taken.

And then ... there was the possibility that they weren't all dead. That some still suffered.

"You shouldn't see this," Alaric repeated, trying to hold her gaze with his. "They're gone, Everin."

The trembles didn't stop. "I need to know how many I killed."

He held her upper arms tight as he searched her face and made her look at him. "Will it matter more if there are more? Will it matter less if there are less?"

Everin closed her eyes as she admitted to herself that it wouldn't. One mangled corpse was enough.

Under a moonless sky, Prince Alaric took her hand.

He led them from the patch of empty gray woods to a new forest. They rode until dawn, and even after that, Tracker passed through a shallow creek before stopping.

They should have been riding to the next settlement. Everin knew this. She also couldn't stop shaking when she'd dropped to the ground after dismounting Tracker.

Everin flexed open and close her hands. These were the hands that had called on a living nightmare.

How could she trust them again?

When his arms found her, she discovered he still carried the smell of woodfire on him. Even though that, too, was a remnant of the ruination that now followed them, she inhaled the smell like it was fresh air.

During a stretch of quiet interrupted only by singing crickets and croaking toads, Everin realized.

That was why the girl had called her a monster. That was why the Guild had so brazenly killed most of the royal family.

It was why they were being hunted down so relentlessly. Why their enemies were so intent on confusing and manipulating them into surrendering.

All for the chance of catching someone who could do *that* in the span of a breath.

In the wrong hands, this could start a war.

Everin was still staring, dazed, at her hands.

"You had no other choice," he murmured in tones as soft as the wind brushing the leaves. His fingers teased out some of her auburn strands that had tangled to her scalp in the night. "It had to be done."

There was nothing to say in response. He held her until the sobs receded, and after, too.

If there was anything Everin still knew, it was that she needed those pages. She needed the ritual to smother her Silverblood—permanently.

If she didn't, it would grow every day that it was allowed to remain a part of her.

A mile of gray, dead forest land would become a settlement.

From a settlement, a kingdom.

CHAPTER SEVEN

In the nights following the incident in the woods, Everin pretended to sleep. This time, she wasn't sure that Alaric knew she was pretending.

What couldn't be ignored was her silence and disinterest. She'd tried, unsuccessfully, to convince him that she was well enough to search another city's book shop or library for the missing pages.

Her voice had sounded hollow even to her.

Everin was holding them back, she knew.

But, for as long as she couldn't answer the question of if she'd use her Silverblood for defense again, she felt she couldn't risk finding out.

As another evening of silence settled in, Alaric abruptly led Tracker away from where they'd been camping at night. They'd been switching where they stayed during the day to get a better idea of if the hunters were on their tail, but so far, they hadn't seen sign of them in the days following their grisly encounter.

Everin blinked. When she spoke, her voice was rough from disuse. "Where are we going?"

He only shook his head. As they neared a copse of spindly trees, he stopped them and dismounted. Their leaves were reddened from the first bite of the cold season, and as the wind shifted, a few left their branches to fall in her hair. He held out a hand for her to come down.

Everin stared at his offered hand.

It shouldn't mean so much to her, but it did.

Alaric didn't have to elaborate why he'd brought Tracker here. He was going to hide the horse and their belongings. Which meant they were leaving their established shelter in these lonely woods.

"You can turn back when you want to," he said in the quiet.

After a few more breaths, Everin dismounted from Tracker. When they touched, her heartrate picked up, though she attempted to hide it.

In hindsight, her easy comments about her finding him attractive sounded silly to her own ears, and she didn't wish to be reminded of them. Even by her own body.

But when she tried to avoid his skin as he helped her down, Alaric only pulled her closer in her descent.

"Before you decide whether or not what you are is a monster—which includes me, incidentally—there's something I need to show you."

Everin froze for a moment before she whispered, "Okay. I'll see it."

They walked through the woods long enough for the sun's rays to stretch through the trees and start to fade by its setting, but a strange thing began to happen.

She noticed it slowly.

The farther from the dying sun they walked, the more the sky brightened. An orange light radiated from beyond the thinning woods they walked. Every once in a while, she could feel Alaric's gaze flick to hers, as if studying her reaction.

The woods finally surrendered to the first few structures of a town she had no name for. Even at this distance, it was clear that crowds of people were wandering about. They were clustered around what looked like street stalls, though these seemed more temporary than the ones they'd seen in Sarshae's streets.

Everin stopped them. Her eyes went to his face, but it was curiously unworried. "Someone could recognize us like this."

"Wait here," Alaric said. He left her for one of the wooden stalls nearby and got in line, his only protection his cloak's hood thrown over his head.

Everin waited for someone to discover him, her hands forming fists as she held them close. Would she be ready to stop the hunters from taking him?

With so many people around, could she do it? Her heart galloped faster. Could she pay with their lives?

Did they deserve to live if it meant that others could die?

But when the prince got to the front, the merchant on the other side of his crates and signs barely spared him another look after Alaric gave him a few coins. He came back to her wearing a half mask. Translucent stones of green and black framed his gold eyes like the scales of a dragon.

Her breath caught. Like this, it was difficult to recognize him.

"Put this on." He handed her another mask, the front of it face-down so she didn't see it. When she tried to turn it over and look at it, he stopped her.

His grin grew more crooked. "Ah, ah. You don't get to see it."

Everin glared at him. She could feel herself blushing, and she tried to cover it up with her annoyance at him.

Good at giving orders, isn't he?

At least this will hide my expression better, she considered, though she didn't mention this out loud either.

Finally, she whispered, "As you wish, *my lord.*"

But it was his reaction that made her want to see the mask most of all. His smirk at her obvious annoyance twitched and fell from his face.

In a voice barely audible, he said, "Everin, you ..."

His gaze went from her eyes to somewhere below them. Her lips.

"You're stunning."

The world felt like it was spinning around her. It didn't seem real, but ... It was clear what he was thinking. At last, she found her voice again.

"Let me see," she whispered back. "I want to see what you chose for me."

Alaric seemed to remember his snark. A smile that could drive a girl to insanity sprang to his lips. "At the end of the night, you can."

"How is that fair?" she wondered, but he was already pulling her further into the heart of the village.

Before they were buried in the crowd, Everin saw the reason for the brightness around them despite the sun having set. Everywhere she looked, lanterns hung from tethers held between poles.

"Is there somewhere we can look for them here?" she asked. Everin didn't want to be overheard talking about the book.

The prince shook his head. "No libraries. No bookshops. Not tonight."

They fell quiet as she watched the people around them. The smell of roasted meat and fruits laced the air, and children traded their favorite foods on sticks with each other.

"Do you know what this is now?" Alaric asked under his breath. They moved closer to the center of the village.

Everin nodded. "I've never been to one, but I've heard of them."

He was watching her again. "What do you know about them?"

"They're held in the southlands where wildfires are common."

"But why do they hold the fire festivals if fire is such a problem here?" he asked her.

In the mass of people, women were handing out pale pink flowers to the other women and girls. One of them pressed a bundle to Everin's hands before she could resist.

"Don't forget to throw them in when the bells go off." The older woman smiled at her. "Unless you're keeping them for your hair."

The woman left them to continue dispersing the flowers to others. Everin stared down at them. They looked like the ones crowding the fields they'd trudged through to get here, though she couldn't be sure.

"I'm not certain," she admitted, finally answering Alaric's question about the festival.

Instead of explaining, he took the flowers' stems and tucked them behind one of her ears. "For later. You'll see."

She looked at him. "Okay. But could you answer something else at least?"

"Am I not an open book?" Prince Alaric asked.

It was her turn to laugh. At his incredulous expression, she said, "The mask. It doesn't help your case."

Everin hadn't realized until then that he'd been leading them to the stalls at the edge of the crowds. Before the nearest one was a small fire contained in a metal pit. Fire-roasted treats smoked on the air.

"What did you want to ask? I'll answer honestly. Promise," he said.

Before she could speak, her stomach spoke for her. Everin looked away from the treats cooking on sticks. "Maybe we should keep moving," she suggested.

They had some coin left from what Alaric had on him when fleeing the castle, but she was well aware of how it wouldn't last forever. Additionally, they couldn't afford the extra risk it would have brought to buy anything unnecessary from merchants in these villages and cities. Most of their diet these days was foraged, aside from a few pieces of butchered meat when they could chance it.

Alaric ignored her and approached the woman running the stall where the sticks were propped before. Like the man selling the festival masks, the woman hardly looked at him once coins were in her possession.

He came back with three sticks between the fingers of each hand. He gave half of them to her. Two were sticks of roasted chicken, and she ate those between bites of four miniature apples skewered through the last stick. The apples were dripping in a spiced honey glaze that the fire had seared into them.

They didn't speak for several minutes until they slowed their chewing. Everin hadn't realized just how hungry she'd been.

"And the question you wanted to ask ...?" the prince ventured as they moved past more stalls.

They'd walked away from those selling food and towards a long line of villagers peddling everything from quilts designed with fire motifs to decorative hanging ornaments.

But her eyes had alighted on one in particular. Hanging from a beam crowded with several other pieces was a tightly woven circle. Dropped from a white string into its middle was a beautiful gemstone of black.

Everin didn't breathe. She'd seen them before, but never after …

Never since becoming a Silverblood.

She felt the hairs on the back of her neck rise.

Do they really work?

Of course not, another voice inside her answered, but she couldn't get her eyes off the stone. In that sense, maybe it already had.

It was an old practice, creating a weard. One she hadn't seen much since her childhood.

Alaric must have seen it at last, for he tried to divert them from the area. But Everin stopped them.

"No. It has to do with my question," Everin said, still staring at the ornament. In a lowered voice, she continued, "I want to know how this proves I'm not a monster."

As if responding to her words, the stone at the center of the weard twisted on its string ever so slightly.

Her throat was dry. In her mind, she saw the mangled bodies again.

Couples meandering around them filed past them one each at a time. Soon, someone would notice her staring and start to wonder. And worry.

As foolish as her obsession probably seemed, she didn't want to lose sight of the weard. She felt that, as soon as she did, its magic would work on her.

The masked dragon beside her tried to pull her forward by her hand. She didn't budge.

Weards were sold to protect a house against the evil of Silverbloods. The stone at the heart of the woven circle signified the most effective weapon humans had against them—Silverblood detectors.

That part was just symbolism. It was the weaver's intent that mattered.

They said that for every weard created, a Silverblood died.

"I can tell you. But only if you let me," he said.

Everin's gaze didn't break from where she stared.

It was more than a trinket. It was evidence that these people, if they really knew her, would hate her. Kill her.

Parents carried them alongside straw dolls in their arms as children raced through the crowds, their spoils forgotten. A girl wearing a mask that reminded her of a snow rabbit blushed when a boy gave her a pocket-sized one with a sparking moonstone at its center.

They must have become more popular since what happened to the king and queen, she realized.

They weren't just ornaments anymore, either. Smaller versions of them were attached to ear clips and pins designed to wear on a hat or shirt.

At last, Everin moved her feet forward. "Tell me."

Prince Alaric surprised her by taking her back to the center of the festival. The villagers had started a bonfire that swirled smoke into the air the size of a raincloud. Combined, the fire from the bonfire and lanterns illuminated the sky as if it were still early evening.

The heat from the fire brushed her skin, and she felt breathless as she watched small sparks dance along the air above it. It was as if the day were motionless in time, stopped at dusk forever.

Behind the glimmering green gems of his mask, the prince stared intently on the fire. There was an expression there that she couldn't quite place.

"From the moment I was born, I was told I was insurance." His voice dipped down almost too low to hear. "The youngest of three heirs. The spare's spare." A sudden, startling laugh rose from his throat, though it died quickly.

"We all had our jobs. Adrian, to learn to be king. Aleksander, to become a good second choice." The prince stared hard at the fire. "Me, to stay quiet behind them. Or at least … that's what my father told me on my tenth birthday."

"I'm sorry. That's a terrible thing for a parent to say." As they spoke, the villagers laughed and danced around them.

He smiled. "But don't you see? That's what made me study harder. Train longer than my brothers. They had years and physical advantages over me."

Prince Alaric closed his fist.

"It's what enabled me to outperform them. Sometimes, I would even hide it. Adrian in particular would get upset."

For many moments, they were silent.

She could see how the memories of his brothers plagued him so. One had been massacred by the Guild on suspicion of being a Silverblood. The other was alive but likely hated Alaric for who he was now.

"But none of that matters anymore," Alaric quietly said, breaking the silence. His gaze slid to her. "We can choose who to be. We can shape—no *carve*—our destiny. This I believe more than anything. You are not just what you are born as. You choose your destiny with every breath."

His gaze was hungry, and the look made her pause.

She slipped her hand into his. Behind them, a bell tolled once, and he moved the flowers from her hair to her hands.

What did she choose?

All around them, folk were tossing them into the bonfire. Everin looked down at her bundle. The flowers were a beautiful, pale pink that dipped into a tinge of orange. But they wouldn't last now that they'd been picked.

"You choose what you are."

Everin was less sure of who she was than ever before. But perhaps that was the point.

She threw them into the fire.

CHAPTER EIGHT

Everin saw the reason for the ritual almost at once. As the wilted flowers took flame, their leaves and petals crisping last in the fire, something released from within the flower.

Seed pods popped into the air, bursting apart from the heat.

"Only by burning them do they release their seeds," Prince Alaric said next to her. "Without the fires, these fields would be bare. You see, these flowers draw crowds of bees every spring to a place otherwise empty of wildflowers. For the people here, their crops are saved by fires."

Everin drew a breath.

Maybe he was right. Maybe this was about who she wanted to be, not who or what she was born as.

A quiet voice inside her mind whispered that maybe he also meant that, kitchen worker or princess, she was the same to him. Her heart galloped at double time as she caught his gaze.

You don't know that, something inside her said, though her heart raced on.

"You never told me what you picked out," she whispered accusingly, pointing to her mask.

"Did I make such a promise? I don't recall." The prince's smirk was rotten enough to spoil a basket of apples.

Everin most definitely remembered a promise. "You liar," she breathed and moved her hand to lift the mask off her face so she could see for herself.

Prince Alaric grabbed her hand suddenly, his grip tight. The realization of what she'd nearly done dawned on her.

She clenched her teeth. She'd nearly given them away. They couldn't afford mistakes like that.

But Alaric wasn't releasing her hand. When she followed his gaze, her stomach dropped.

They were working their way through the crowds, their red cloaks like tongues of flame risen from ashes.

They'd found them.

"Follow me." Alaric's voice was strained but quiet. His face betrayed no alarm, and Everin fought to keep hers as neutral as possible, too.

He pulled her by the hand through the crowd, careful not to appear bothered by the sight. The villagers around them paid them or the hunters little heed as they continued dancing and merrymaking.

Would that change soon?

Would the mage hunters announce that a Silverblood was in the area?

It would create mass panic. They can't risk it, she thought.

As beautiful a tribute as the great bonfire was, it would be dangerous if objects or other people were pushed too close to it in the hysteria.

Though she tried not to stare and appear suspicious, Everin couldn't help but search for them through the crowds when she could. As she caught glimpses of the hunters, she started to see.

They were stopping people here and there, asking to remove their masks or festival costumes.

Her heartbeat thundered faster.

"Should we run?" Her voice was nearly inaudible.

A subtle, stiff shake of his head was all the answer she got, and she saw the reason for it after a moment. The mage hunters and their horses were blocking the main entry into the village.

They *couldn't* run.

As they passed the tables and stalls where vendors sold their wares, the prince's wrist flicked back to grab something off one, though the movement was too quick for her to see what it was.

Finally, Alaric slowed as they reached a canopied stall bigger than the others they'd passed so far. Except, no one was working at this one.

The night air played with the fringes of her dress along her legs, bringing in air warmer than was seasonal. Even so, a chill rose on her skin.

He led her inside, and she saw at once that she'd been mistaken. This was not a stall for selling woven trinkets or bonfire food.

Baskets and baskets of flowers were piled around them. Their honeyed scent saturated the air and filled her lungs. They were the same pale pink flowers that grew in the fields around the village.

Just past the stall, she saw a band of red push through the crowd, the light from their lanterns bright against the rest of the festival's flames.

"You'll need these." The prince passed her two small objects.

Everin drew breath when she saw what they were. She almost recoiled just from holding them.

"I don't understand." Her heart hammered faster. The mage hunters were nearly to them.

"Do you trust me?" In the darkness, his eyes almost passed for a light brown. She couldn't breathe when he looked at her like that.

"Of course."

She was already fastening one of the metal clips to her ear lobe when his hand went to her jaw. "Let me," he whispered at her neck.

Everin could feel the tiny woven strands brush against her skin as he clasped the weard earrings to her ears. When he was done, his hand hovered at her neck.

"Stay still," he ordered.

She did as he said—not even daring a nod—though her heart wouldn't obey as it thrashed inside her chest. He tilted her neck back, holding her in place with one hand against a wooden post.

His lips brushed against her skin too tenderly, and she nearly broke her word then. Her pulse ran fast enough to make her dizzy as she tried to understand everything that was happening.

The Guild was coming for them, but her heart seemed to care more about the fact that his hands were on her. Heat built inside her as he traced a vein under her skin.

Alaric pressed his mouth to her ear. "Play along for our lives," he whispered before moving her to face him again.

Like the masks they wore, this was another kind of mask, Everin realized. They needed to seem like two young lovers caught in a tryst away from the brightness of the festival. For, if the mage hunters stopped too long to look at them, if they thought them anything other than two fools in love, they would pay with their lives.

"Yes," she breathed, but it was caught in the kiss he planted on her lips.

Everin's desire to live mixed up with her feelings for the prince, and she felt as if she were lost among a wide sea. Her heart beat faster and faster, though her hands froze at her sides.

Move, she ordered her limbs, but they stayed where they were.

Prince Alaric pressed himself against her, his torso pinning hers against him and the post. Her body finally picked up the suggestion and one of her hands moved in order to better kiss him, but, as fast as a snake striking for a mouse, his free hand locked her wrist in his grip.

In her mind she said his name, over and over.

Dizziness came, forcing Everin to pull back from their kiss.

"Are you ready?" Alaric whispered under his breath. A flicker of the hunters' lights flashed just past their tent. The sound of gravel crunching under their boots disturbed the chorus of faraway laughter.

The look in his eyes stole her breath. She nodded instead of speaking, though she felt far from ready.

This is just for show. We have to sell this farce or be hunted.

But something in her heart—her body—didn't believe it.

Prince Alaric's hand darted out as fast as it had before, and a *rip* broke their silence. She felt the touch of his fingers brush against her bare skin as he perfectly positioned the ripped part in the chest of her dress.

He intercepted her glance down at herself, holding her chin with his finger. "A swan doesn't need to check her reflection."

Her cheeks warmed as she realized he was referring to the mask he'd picked out for her. *That* part hadn't been for show ... had it?

Before Everin could decide, the prince's lips were on hers again, his hand against her throat to hold her steady against him.

At the last moment, she remembered to act as if they'd been kissing the whole time rather than purposefully ripping her dress. She moved her free hand to lock her fingers in his hair as a voice called out on their other side.

"That's enough. Unless you'd like to share."

As their kiss broke, Everin's gaze whipped past her view of Alaric to catch sight of them.

Her pulse pounded hard enough to nearly be heard. There were about a half dozen of them, their swords all gleaming against their flickering lanterns.

Briefly, the flame illuminated the face of the one in front. He wore glasses that slid down his nose as he looked at them. Slightly, he tilted his head to glance back at the one who had apparently spoken earlier.

"Yes, that's quite enough. Perhaps you'd be better off shoveling after the horses than helping me."

When that elicited no response from the other hunter, Everin realized that, despite the youth of this one, he was their leader. And, as he stepped forward, she realized another thing as flamelight flickered across more of him.

Carefully hidden under the layers of his red coat and Guild tunic was an array of bandages that stretched to the top of his chest. He'd been heavily injured recently.

He was among the ones chasing us through the forests outside of this village. Everin nearly jolted up.

She'd thought there'd been no survivors.

"Although, he is right." The hunter with glasses stepped forward again. One side of his lips twisted a tad as if he smelled something off in the air. "What are you doing here? Who are you?"

Alaric turned so that she was half-shielded to them and spoke in a voice she'd never heard, "Does that need an answer? We wanted privacy." He tilted his head towards the throng of people in the center of the festival. His chest was still moving up and down too quickly from their kiss.

The light from their lanterns passed over his face where green stones made for scales in his mask. A little closer, and the flames couldn't fail to show his golden eyes, a trait only the royal line had. They weren't playing with fire—they were bathing in it.

What if they have Silverblood detectors? What if they're just toying with us?

Everin couldn't shake the feeling.

Their leader's eyes narrowed slightly. "Fair enough. But ..." He stepped to the side, his high boots leaving gravel for dirt. He turned his head back to the rest of his party. "Dorian. Search them." Behind his glasses, his eyes moved back to Everin. "Her first."

One of the others—thankfully not the one who'd made the initial comment—strode forward and gestured her to the side.

She felt her legs move as if they were a puppet's. It was clear to her how his eyes flicked from one part of her to another.

First the tear in her dress. Next her mask. Then the weard earrings.

Finally, they settled on the wool cap that she wore to keep her recognizable hair hidden.

Whispers started inside her head again, telling her to use the power that slept inside her.

What's the difference in using it then and now? We were fleeing for our lives before.

It's only a matter of minutes before they discover who we are in this tent.

The Silver ran through her veins, urging her to use it. Whose bodies would be left behind this time?

The hunters' ... or theirs?

And then there were the people at the festival just paces from them.

Could she use it to save their lives when it meant endangering everyone in the area?

"Mask off then your cap," Dorian the mage hunter ordered. "We need to see the full faces of everyone here. A monster may be lurking in the area."

Out of her periphery, she saw something in Alaric's sleeve. When she hadn't looked, he must have slipped it from where it'd been hidden on his body to the underside of his palm. His eyes met with hers.

The Silverblood in her thrashed faster. Prince Alaric had already decided to try to fend the hunters off without the use of their cursed magic, but she wasn't so sure they'd make it out alive this way, either.

Their time was up. Everin's hands moved to the mask at her face, though she wasn't so sure of what she'd do next.

Would she be the monster and stop their enemies completely?

Or would she be the helpless girl who could barely fight off these men with wandering eyes and poison words?

"You choose what you are."

Everin stared out at the deep night sky beyond the orange glow at the village's heart. Anywhere close to the light of the bonfire, and it would be too close to people.

What if it doesn't work? What if it grows much bigger than I intend?

Her hands shook, and the mage hunter snapped at her, "Hurry it up. Or you'll be coming with us for non-compliance with Guild business."

Everin's knees buckled, and she lost her balance as she slid into the baskets of flowers piled behind her. But her interrogator, Dorian, didn't seem to notice.

Everin saw it first because her sight was concentrated on the spot, though the others twisted to look almost immediately from the odd change in the air.

It was strange. It didn't make a sound, though they must have all felt it when it happened to have turned so quickly. A blast of Silver bloomed in the sky just outside bounds of the village, sending small strands of silver fading from its center.

Though she'd been successful, her stomach curled into itself to see it.

The reaction of the mage hunters was almost as instantaneous as the blast had been. In a blink, everything from their postures to their words changed.

This was what they'd been trained and bred for.

Their weapons fell into their hands almost as if they'd always been there.

They were quiet all except for one mutter. It rose the hairs on the back of her neck.

"The Guildmaster's meter didn't show that."

Their leader, the boy with glasses, seemed to ignore the whisper as his gaze snapped forward. "Dorian and Harlock, in front with me. The rest will divide and flank the target. Remember protocol for innocents."

He stopped and glanced back at her and the prince as his team surged past him. "Stay where you are for your own safety. Don't trust those not in red."

But a funny thing happened then. Even as the other mage hunters sprinted to mount their horses and stop the apparent attack on the village, he didn't budge.

Instead, he was still. His gaze lingered on Alaric's dragon mask.

Something twisted again at the edge of his mouth as it had when he'd seen them for the first time.

He knows. He knows it's the prince.

CHAPTER NINE

When they found Tracker again, they rode through the night. As they raced past trees and moonlit fields, Everin felt that every shadow and crevice held their enemies. Her body was wired for a fight even as she prayed that Tracker would take them someplace no person had ever been.

Behind her, Alaric was silent too. She assumed he was, like her, replaying every moment that had nearly led to their discovery.

Including the parts where they'd kissed.

It felt as if Everin had left her heart somewhere behind her, as if it were too slow to catch up with her body. Or maybe it was that her body was too slow for her heart.

But when the prince finally spoke, his voice was low with a strange-sounding emotion running underneath it.

"Have you ever done something like that before?"

Everin's cheeks heated. She'd had a few flings with boys in the past—a stableboy, a cook, and a cobbler.

Never a prince, she added in her mind.

"Maybe once or twice." Her voice was a whisper. "But not like that."

Never *like that.*

It was then that she looked behind her to see his face and realized her mistake. She'd assumed he'd been thinking of their kiss. But he was looking down where the Book of Dissimulation was strapped to his body.

A second later, he met her eyes. "That blast. That was …" His eyes drifted from hers. "I never thought it could be used at a distance."

Everin bit down her tongue to give her something to focus on other than her raging, embarrassed heart.

For him, their kiss had only been a deceit meant to trick the hunters.

Of course, she corrected herself. *That's what it always was.*

"Is something wrong?"

She shook her head. Everin didn't trust her voice now. It might betray her like her heart had.

A moment later, he spoke again. "We need to go to the capital city."

Everin stared straight ahead. Her breath was lost on the air as Tracker pummeled the earth beneath them.

She'd been there before when her ma had still been alive. It was a sprawling, large city that served as the heart of the kingdom of Aurus, a place where roads crossed and spiderwebbed forth.

It was also the closest city to the Guild's headquarters and informally ran by Guild captains. From what she remembered of the place, there were officials in red on every corner.

"If they find us anywhere," she said, still staring forward, "they'll find us there."

Alaric was quiet for so long that she wasn't sure if he were going to respond at all. Then, he said, "It's the only place left that might have it. The only city left with a bookshop that trades in uncommon books."

He added a second later, "I have no more leads. We have to do it."

In her heart, she knew he was right. They couldn't keep this life up, whether that was the part where they were constantly hiding or the part where they were putting others' lives in danger with the power that raged inside them.

But why is it that our efforts to find the pages seem to only draw our enemies closer to us?

There was a feeling in the pit of her stomach that she couldn't ignore. One that whispered they were steps away from falling into the Guild's traps once and for all.

Her thoughts came to her more clearly then, and she realized then what was bothering her.

"It feels almost as if ... as if they know what we're trying to do. I think it's what's kept them on our trail since Sarshae." Everin swallowed. Once she'd started talking, the words were coming looser now, her earlier embarrassment not forgotten but put aside.

"So, I think we should hide for a few days. We need more food and supplies, anyway, and in the meantime maybe we can find a better way to disguise ourselves before we try to go inside the capital city."

The prince was silent again for many minutes.

"Everin. Every moment that this is inside us, it grows stronger. What happens when we're nothing but vessels for it?" He touched her cheek.

Her ears were burning. Of course he was right. The vision of what she'd done just a few days ago was still burnt into her mind.

As was their kiss. Everin stared ahead, not daring to open her mouth and embarrass herself further.

It was just a disguise. Just like the masks.

Then why didn't her heart seem to think so?

CHAPTER TEN

After Prince Aleksander shook the hand of the last diplomat standing between him and the door that would separate him from the public eye for longer than the length of a piss, he screamed.

Or rather, in his mind, he screamed.

Because, on the other side of the door to his private room, was yet another Guild captain.

"If you haven't found him yet, you have nothing to say to me," Aleksander managed, his right hand already on the hilt of his sword.

"Aleksander. I'm sorry I couldn't be at the funeral."

Aleksander stepped closer and saw that who he'd taken to be another Guild prick was actually Vaun.

Behind his glasses, his eyes held a kind of sorrow that a person could only have for a friend. Immediately, Aleksander collapsed into a chair at the table where Vaun sat.

His High Knight, ever his silent shadow, moved wordlessly to block the room's only window. He hadn't spoken since the funeral except to threaten officials and diplomats here and there, and he didn't speak now.

"It's fine," Aleksander said, though nothing felt *fine* anymore. His gaze snapped to a detail he hadn't noticed on Vaun yet. Pinned to the top of his cloak was the reason he'd taken him to be a random Guild captain in the first place. A captain's badge.

And there, underneath his Guild cloak and tunic, was a crossing of bandages.

Aleksander pieced it together at once. Vaun was good, but for too long he'd been just under the rank of Guild captain. A spot had opened up above him.

Which was a nice way of saying a Silverblood had murdered his superior.

Sick creatures. His nails dug into the worn wood of the table.

This changed things. "I heard about the attack north of Firefields. I didn't realize you were involved," Aleksander said.

His pulse picked up. This was exactly what he needed.

Since the attack on the castle and his family, Aleksander had fought for answers as to exactly what had happened.

So far, all he'd gotten was silence from the Guild and a sea of beggars, liars, and thieves in the form of his father's advisors. No one wanted to cause the people to panic. But that meant no one wanted to talk, either.

"Vaun. You know what I need to hear."

His friend's eyes swept to his. "And you know this is venturing into Guild business."

Aleksander leaned closer. "Then consider it *personal* business."

"Aleks." Vaun moved his fingers behind his glasses to rub his eyes. "It's not that I don't want to. I'm on orders."

"Then why are you here, waiting for me all alone in my room?" He stared forward at his friend, quite aware that he was probably losing him as a friend by acting this way.

Something in him couldn't seem to care.

When Vaun didn't respond, Aleksander got out of his seat and started pacing.

"Then you tell me if I've lost it. Tell me if I'm out of my mind for thinking there's something suspicious about a Silverblood assassinating the royal family but no one can show me the last body. Tell me I'm crazy for wanting to see it even if it's just bits."

His fists tightened and he stopped to face the other wall like he was talking to it and not Vaun.

All the rage, disgust, regret, and pain from the last couple weeks funneled through him like a water spout.

His father's face. His mother's. Already cold by the time he'd gotten there. He breathed.

"I just want to know." Aleksander's eyes closed. His voice cut down until it was barely audible. "I need to know if it's true. If Alaric is dead, too."

They'd told him the Silverblood had likely killed him, too. *But there had never been a body.*

When the silence stretched on, Aleksander walked to the door leading out of his suite. His High Knight followed like a shadow. Though he could never truly be alone anymore, he would find some other place to sleep tonight.

"You're right. You deserve to hear it straight."

At Vaun's words, Aleksander turned. He had produced something from one of his pockets. It was a scroll holder that, when he popped open one side of it, let out a many-folded piece of parchment instead of a scroll.

Vaun continued to speak. "The others—the Guildmaster in particular—might disagree with the timing of releasing this information, but at this rate you're going to hear about it soon enough."

He met his friend's gaze. Did he want to know the truth?

Finally, he decided that he'd spent too long without it. Prince Aleksander walked forward and read the paper.

And he read it again. And again.

Aleksander was about to destroy it when Vaun snatched it back from him. It tumbled back into its container, though Aleksander's eyes didn't leave the spot where it must have rested inside.

"You can see why this wasn't made public." Vaun's voice was quiet.

"Is he alive." Aleksander's voice was lower. "Have you seen him."

"You have to realize this whole abduction business may be a trap. That you knowing this puts your life in further danger," Vaun said.

"Is he alive," Aleksander repeated.

Slowly, Vaun nodded.

It was all Aleksander needed to know. He had a monster to hunt.

In his pocket was a picture of a girl with fire-red hair. Vaun claimed that they couldn't approach her for fear that she would kill her hostage.

Good thing Aleksander had other ways of working than the Guild did.

CHAPTER ELEVEN

Everin's hand grazed the spines, the leather of the bindings pleasant to her touch. The oil lamp nearest this shelf cast a wavering light over everything. Her eyes scanned the wall of books. Despite herself—despite the danger they were in, coming to the capital city so soon after nearly being caught—she smiled.

So far, Alaric had been right. It seemed as though the Guild didn't expect their presence so near their headquarters. He'd bought her a new wool cap that hid most all of her hair and new clothes from the dress she'd trudged around in.

She'd snuck into the city by herself with the dockworkers at daybreak. Everin had even had time to buy a loaf of bread for them. After a few small bites, she'd folded it away in her pack.

No one had given her a second glance. It was *working*.

Her hand flicked back the spine of one particularly worn-looking book, and she rescued it from where it had been shoved among the others. The writing on the front was embossed in loops and curves, and the pages inside were light and papery.

Everin liked to pretend she could read them.

She should be leaving. She'd already passed the note to the bookseller at the desk, and he'd already informed her that he hadn't even heard of what she was seeking.

"Can I help you?"

Before her was the bookseller, the one that had taken one look at the note Alaric had written and refuted the very existence of the book that they possessed.

She knew from Alaric what the note said. She carried the same one to every bookshop and library they'd visited.

She was an assistant to a collector of rare and forgotten books, searching on his behalf for the missing pages of the infamous Book of Dissimulation. They didn't claim to have the book itself, which Alaric had explained would have been too risky a claim to make, even if most would have laughed at the idea.

Everin's palm shoved the spine of the book back among its fellows as she blurted, "No, thank you. I was browsing, but I should be going now."

There was a strange look to the book merchant's eyes that made Everin want to drop the pretense of civility between them and leave without another word.

The memory of the librarian who had recognized her shot through Everin. She needed to leave now.

This one was only a few years older than her. Most of the book merchants in other towns had been plying their trade for so many years that they needed the thickest spectacles that Everin had ever seen in her life in order to see. It made her grateful that she'd never learned to read.

In a voice that was at once a whisper and much too rough to be called such, he said, "Do you know what it is you're looking for?"

Breath stuck in her throat. She said, "Of course. But seeing as you don't have it—"

"You can't read, can you?"

Everin's sweat-coated back pressed against the stacks. She regretted ever picking up a book in this shop.

"That's none of your business," she said between her teeth.

"You know the basics," he said in his grating not-whisper, "Some letters, perhaps."

"That's got nothing to do with—"

"Where is he?"

Something cold solidified in her stomach. Her eyes moved about the shop. She knew the mage hunters would materialize at any moment.

They'd been discovered.

Again.

The merchant's eyes were unreadable as they watched her reaction. "Where is your book collector master?"

Breath released from her. Maybe he *didn't* realize who they were. Maybe he thought she was a simple errand girl and assistant, after all. They appeared to be alone in the shop, but Everin kept her knuckle near the dagger hidden at the inside of her trousers.

She didn't relax. Whatever this bookseller was intending, it couldn't have been benign.

Her eyes narrowed at him. "He's close by," she said in what she hoped sounded like a threat.

His reaction unnerved her. The bookseller stepped back from her, acting as if he hadn't interrogated her against the book stacks seconds earlier.

He nodded. "I see I misunderstood your request, madam. Allow me to search through our special collections."

Everin hadn't relaxed by the time the young bookseller had returned, and she didn't budge when he'd tried to exchange her money for a string-tied envelope.

With some force, he'd shoved it into her closed fist.

"Thank you for your business. I would highly suggest you check the contents yourself before passing them to your master. I'm sure you wouldn't want to incur his wrath by presenting to him the wrong thing."

Everin was gone from the shop before he could say another thing to her. Despite the warmth on her skin from the sun overhead and the smells of cooking meat and bread that she loved about civilization, her heart raced.

She hadn't been exactly truthful when she'd told him that Alaric was close by, but what of the bookseller's reaction?

What had any of it meant?

As she raced through the cobbled streets of the town, her eyes flew to every alleyway and passerby who happened to glance at her.

The mage hunters would have started after her by now if he'd have known who she was, she assured herself. But she couldn't force herself to stop looking for them in every face and shadow.

Her thumb smoothed out the rough paper material of the envelope. This bookseller had been the most peculiar by far.

But did that mean he was dangerous?

"I'm sure you wouldn't want to incur his wrath by presenting to him the wrong thing."

Everin shook her head. She should have been drunk on giddiness, but her apprehension wouldn't let her release the feeling that she was being hunted even now.

There was no book collector master. There was no wrath to incur.

Either the envelope in her hand contained one of the missing pages or it didn't.

And what if it doesn't?

This was their last solid lead, according to Alaric.

Either way, we're leaving this city behind, she reminded herself. Everin didn't breathe as she passed a figure in a red cloak.

She timed her steps to her breaths so that they weren't too fast. It was a challenge not to duck and run through the crowd meandering the streets.

Was he watching her? Did he have a detector device?

Alaric said that, if he noticed a disturbance within the city, he'd try the technique she'd used at the fire festival and use his Silverblood over an uninhabited area to distract any hunters.

"You can't read, can you?"

Everin's lips pressed together as heat rushed to her cheeks where the sun had already warmed them.

What did that matter?

But how had he known?

Her knees started to weaken as she approached the edge of the city. Here, the gates didn't lock at sundown and she had plenty of time to slip through them.

Soon, she would find Alaric on the other side of them. She'd tell him how odd the bookseller had acted, and they'd laugh over these people with their noses glued to books. They'd eat the rest of the loaf once they stopped again.

And maybe, just maybe, they'd discover that she'd found one of the pages they needed to save themselves.

And if they didn't, it wasn't as if he'd be upset with her.

It would be difficult, but they'd continue. They'd find another bookshop or library or curio store.

One of her canines hooked into her tongue. Her eyes rested on the horizon before her. Her body continued to walk straight as her brain instructed it, but one of her hands worked independently of the rest of her.

Inside the envelope, she found two slips of paper.

CHAPTER TWELVE

For the first few days, Alaric had been inseparable from the page, bent over it while he tended to the coals of their fire.

Everin wasn't sure why she hadn't shown him the second piece of paper the bookseller had slipped her.

After all, it wasn't as if she could read it. Not really, anyway.

What if it's the last page of the book?

But she'd already assured herself otherwise.

One of the papers had yellowed from age, and although she couldn't understand what was written on it, Everin had recognized the flourish of the letters as the same style that the rest of the book had.

But the other piece of parchment was newly written. Some of the ink had even smudged when it had been folded and placed inside the envelope.

The bookseller had written the note for her.

Her mouth came down. He had recognized that she wasn't literate.

So, the bookseller was mocking her.

The knowledge was enough to sour the feeling that had soared in her at seeing Alaric's face when she'd presented him the page.

She'd hidden the note in her pocket like she could hide away everything that made her so different from the prince. She ran her fingers roughly through her tangles. For some reason, she felt that princess hair must not tangle.

Prince Alaric's regular breathing from where he laid beside her tickled her. She watched how the moonlight poured across his features.

When the ritual worked—and they were both free of the Silverblood that marked them for death—what then?

Would he go back to being a prince? Would she go back to washing dishes in too-warm kitchens, somewhere far from where she'd be recognized?

Or would they carve out a life like this—and leave their former lives behind, together on Tracker's back? Could someone like him be content with someone like her?

Somehow, neither scenario seemed right to her.

Her thumb slipped inside her pocket, and she retrieved the note. Maybe she couldn't change the fact that she'd grown up on rotted apples and molded bread. She couldn't change who she had been.

She could change who she was.

She could be closer to his equal.

Everin slipped from under their shared quilt closer to their fire. Against its dying light, her eyes traced the curves and lines until they ached.

The flickering sounds of the flame muffled the sounds she made with her mouth as it formed shapes she'd nearly forgotten.

****

When morning light pierced the sky above, she hadn't slept.

Or, she didn't think she had. But she also didn't remember moving their pack from where it hung in the trees.

She discovered it not placed where they usually put it, tied to a branch just above their heads and, hopefully, the heads of any bears, but lodged much higher in the tree than where she'd left it.

Alaric was still sleeping when she'd gone to retrieve it for the day of riding ahead of them. It wasn't as if an animal had gotten to it because it wasn't torn apart on the ground as she'd have expected.

Instead, it had been untied and then placed higher in the tree between a particularly thick branch and the trunk.

Everin's skin crawled. It felt too much like a trap.

Run back. Run back and get Alaric and get out of here.

But the only sounds around her were of the woods waking to a new day. Birdsong above her. Crickets scattered through the area. A crisp chill clung to the leaves below her.

She would have heard anyone following her, she told herself.

Before she decided to, Everin had started to climb the tree to get their supplies down. It was their habit to hide their pack about a mile from where they camped. This way, if they ever got separated, they had a mutual point to return to that was a fair distance from where they camped.

As she pulled herself to where their pack had been moved to in the tree, she saw something that made her stomach turn with a sickness. Everin's hold on the branches nearly gave.

From here, she could distantly see Alaric beginning to rise from sleep and prepare their breakfast over a low fire.

Someone was tracking them. And this time, they weren't merely trying to capture or kill them.

A slip of paper had fallen from within their bag to her lap. The paper had been ripped, but she recognized it all the same.

It was one identical to the notice she'd seen in the Sarshae library. But this one had been torn along her neck in the picture.

The drawing of her face stared lifelessly back up at her.

Someone was toying with them.

When she got back, Alaric had stared at the torn picture for many minutes of silence. Everin had told him everything—everything except her encounter with the bookseller and his note.

After this morning, that seemed much less important now.

"I don't understand. Why—" She couldn't complete the thought, but it hung in the air between them.

Why my picture?

Alaric crumpled the paper in his fist. "The Guild likes to play games. This feels too much like them not to be their doing." His gaze shot to hers. "They're trying to split us up. They know how powerful two Silverbloods can be together."

But Everin couldn't stop pacing.

What did it mean? The mage hunter from the festival had let them go. She *knew* he had. And now this ...

"What are we going to do?" Everin's hand hadn't left the knife at her waist. How could they escape now? This person had watched them camp and sleep and done nothing. "They found us before. They could probably kill us at any time they want." With each word, her voice had strained tighter and tighter through her throat.

"And yet they haven't. Listen to me, Everin." As he said her name, he stopped her pacing with his arm on hers. He moved her face so that she had no choice but to look into his eyes. "They're trying to draw us to them, but we won't fall for that."

His touch sent a jolt through her. "We can do this. Together, we can save ourselves."

"Okay," she exhaled, her eyes moving down to her hands. It helped her breathing when she looked away from his face. "It's just—they're getting close. Too close."

"Yes. You're right. We have to start the ritual," Alaric said. "It's our only chance to get out of their snare." She felt his eyes on her. "As soon as we null the curse inside us, we stop being useful to them, and they'll give it up."

But the longer Everin stared at the healed-over scar on her hand where she'd drawn the magic from her veins, the more she wondered if this ritual would work at all.

She'd been shown that magic existed.

Now that it was out, what if it wouldn't leave?

And what if this nightmare doesn't stop when it does?

Chapter Thirteen

The ritual would be tonight.

It had taken them two more days to acquire all that was needed for it. They were still one page short, but Alaric had puzzled out that the missing pages detailed not one ritual but two—or two stages of the same one.

After this part, the Silverblood within them would be dulled. The second part of the ritual would snuff it from their veins entirely. According to Alaric, their blood may even pass for red after the first part was complete.

But Everin worried what would happen if they never found the second page.

It was beginning to feel more and more likely.

Though they seemed to have lost their hunters, Everin felt able to do little else but worry and watch for their enemies. Between Tracker resting and eating, they'd ridden almost the whole time of the last couple of days. As night fell again and they had to stop riding for lack of light, she couldn't help but startle at everything from the wind moving the branches overhead to her own boots squeaking under her. While Alaric had already searched a wide radius around them to ensure they were alone, her heart didn't seem to listen to logic.

Water for their cooking pot sloshed on the front of her blue-gray dress, and she hissed under her breath. Her other clothes, the shirt and trousers, were hanging by the fire to dry.

"What's wrong?" Alaric was by her side at once, abandoning the book where he'd been studying it to prepare for the ritual.

"It's just—Nothing." Everin shook her head rather than try to explain. "I'm fine."

Alaric looked at her and appeared to see right through her. His mouth formed a thin line.

"You're nervous." All at once, Everin felt a warm hand cup her chin. Her heart stuttered in her ribs. "That's natural." His gold eyes left her face, but it didn't help her heartrate. "I am, too."

Even though she wanted this more than anything, she couldn't get herself to speak or even nod. Her pulse was like a hammer against brittle ribs, and she felt herself shaking.

"Everin," he breathed, and the sound sent chills through her. His eyes narrowed. "What's going on? Really?"

"I'm afraid." Everin stared out beyond their hidden camp, into the forest beyond them.

"This will work. I'm sure of it," Alaric said. After a moment, he amended, "I will *make* sure of it."

But her eyes hadn't left the forest. Her voice lowered. "And what if this is the only thing keeping us safe?"

And ... what if I'm nothing to you after this?

After I'm plain again?

She hadn't been able to admit these thoughts even to herself until then, but the thought had holed through her heart like a worm through fruit.

"They won't have reason to touch us once we're done. We'll be free of them," he said. "They can't touch a prince or any member of the royal family unless it goes against the laws on Silvers."

"A prince," Everin whispered and then stopped.

Prince Alaric watched her in silence for long enough to make her cheeks heat. She felt that her thoughts showed too much on her face.

"A prince. Right," he said, his eyes elsewhere, too. Finally, he said, "Wait here."

Alaric went back to their pack, digging until he was apparently satisfied by something. He came back, though she didn't see anything different.

That was, until he opened his palm.

Everin drew a breath.

She'd never seen real diamonds, and two large, very real ones gazed back. They dangled like teardrops from where a lady would fix them to her ears.

"Throughout my family, these have been worn by the ruling queen. As you can figure, they were my mother's," he said in a lower voice. He caught her gaze. "I want you to have them. I want you to wear them for this."

"I couldn't." She stepped back. But her heart thrummed out a different answer.

He stepped forward. "Everin. You were meant to wear these. You were meant to be here with me." Finally, he closed the gap between them completely.

"You were meant to be with me," he whispered.

His voice sent chills along her skin. She didn't move as his fingers probed along her neck until they stopped at one of her ears. Carefully, he clasped one to her ear.

Everin barely managed to speak, "How can that be?"

"I'll show you how." As he spoke, a devilish smirk twisted his lips.

The diamond teardrop was cold against her skin as he moved her head in the opposite direction to access her other ear. But, before he put it on her, his mouth appeared at the base of her collarbone.

Everin gasped, the crisp evening air almost burning her throat.

He stopped, speaking against her skin. "Now. How do I convince you that tonight, you are completely and utterly mine? That every worry—every thought, in fact—is in vain?"

Does he mean it?

Her memories of the fire festival ran through her mind—the feel of his hands on her, the smell and taste of him, and how he locked his eyes on her.

It all came rushing back.

Maybe it wasn't pretend.

Everin's cheeks burned. Words braver than her poured out of her mouth. "I guess you'll have to prove it to me."

Alaric's hand slipped against the back of her head to hold her against him. His mouth trailed kisses up her throat until he got to her face.

"What are you feeling right now?" he asked her, his eyes on her lips.

"I feel like," she swallowed. She felt like she felt *too much*. Finally, she added, "I feel like I'm in a dream."

His smile became sharper. "That's because you are."

Alaric's finger moved under her chin to pull her face to his, and she was.

CHAPTER FOURTEEN

"*You were meant to be with me.*"

Everin's pulse ran through her hard enough to make her dizzy.

The light of the dawn sun caught on the knife's blade, highlighting the cold, polished metal that had cut her once already.

What had happened last night had seemed too much like a dream to be true, but unlike for the girls in fairy tale stories, the prince in her story hadn't turned to dust in the morning light.

Her face reddened when she thought on it, though she tried to concentrate on her task. Everin was gathering the supplies they would need for the ritual: an empty glass container, her knife, and some bandages.

But her mind was still on what had happened last night and what it meant for them.

Had he really meant what he'd said?

Her heart jumped a beat at the possibility.

Was it really more than a night together?

She'd shared the night with boys before. Those had been nights of mutual comfort where each of them had known where they stood. And, importantly, that they would part ways come morning.

Those nights, she'd held no hopeful delusions that the other person felt something deeper for her. Even if the morning after came a little colder than usual, there was a strange solace in the knowing.

A breath brushed against her shoulder as hands tightened around her waist.

"How does it feel being the property of the crown prince's?"

A familiar warmth fluttered inside her like her erratic heartbeat. Yes, that most certainly *hadn't* been a dream, she decided.

She should have turned around and kissed him then, but, in her confusion, the words tumbled out of her mouth before she could stop them.

"Crown prince?"

The phrase *crown prince* was usually reserved for the heir, rather than one of the younger princes.

He appeared to notice his misspoken words seconds after she did because his grip on her changed from urgent to nonexistent.

"Right. Nevermind that." He sighed as he pulled away from her.

Everin turned on her heels. "What's wrong?"

Before he could turn back to his notes and the torn page, she stopped him. "Alaric. Talk to me, please."

Alaric stared at the words on the page below him as he spoke. "I forgot." He didn't look up as he continued. "I forgot which of my brothers lived and which died."

His words to her about his remaining brother came back to Everin then.

"It's possible he yet lives, Alaric. That the Guild hasn't gotten to him yet. Perhaps if you contact him, he would help us."

"He wouldn't accept it." Alaric had formed a fist as he spoke. "Aleksander would kill me on the spot."

"I'm sorry," she whispered.

His only answer was to shake his head.

Would it have been worse if he'd lost his entire family or that one of them remained, only to hate Alaric for what he'd become?

He was staring at her when she looked at him again. He asked, "Are you sure you're up for this?"

Everin seriously considered it.

She'd saved them more than once using the curse inside her.

But it wouldn't have been necessary in the first place if we didn't carry it inside our blood, she considered.

It was time she reached for the future she was keeping locked in her dreams. It was time to face her fears and stop running.

Finally, she said, "Only if you are."

He caught her gaze as he walked towards her. His eyes were a magnetic gold. "More than ever." He pushed some of her hair behind her ear.

She swallowed drily, trying to calm her raging heart. Everin stared at her hands. It was easier to look at them than him.

"I want to do it," she whispered. "Start the ritual."

He led her by the hand to a low stump on the ground near their cold fire where she'd left the supplies he'd asked her to gather.

"Do you trust me?"

His strange gold eyes were on her. She heard her mouth answer for her.

"Yes."

Alaric's palm pulled away from her, and she resisted the urge to bring it back to her. He rifled through the sack on the ground before producing a sharp knife, the one she kept on her when she travelled inside towns and villages.

In his other hand was the glass flask.

"I'll need to collect some blood," he said.

She heard what he meant, and she didn't correct him. Everin nodded and allowed Prince Alaric's careful fingers to face her palm sunward. When the slice of pain came, she bit down on her lip and closed her eyes.

She didn't have blood anymore. She didn't need to see it coming out of her to know.

Alaric wrapped a bandage tight around her hand after.

When she opened her eyes, he was examining the flask in his fist. "Some of mine's in here, as well." His golden eyes flicked to her face. "I need you to stay still for this part."

Alaric's thumb stoppered the top of the glass as he flipped it upside down. Although he tried to hide it, Everin saw him flinch when it must've made contact with his thumb. The skin came away silver.

Everin didn't dare breathe. His thumb traced lines on her face.

All she could think about was his hands on her the night before, and bumps raised on her skin despite the warmth of the sun on her.

When he was done, he repeated it on his own features, sweeping his thumb from his nose to his lip and around his eyes.

Hers felt like tears wet on her cheekbones.

"Are you ready?"

She gave a nod, though nothing could have prepared her for his palm pressing against her skin. His longest finger rested under her collarbone.

Her pulse pounded at the contact. She was certain he could feel her heartbeat.

He spoke to the empty forest around them. "I call on the Silverblood—"

It was all he could say before the ground rumbled and the winds drowned out his words. Everything shuddered as what appeared to be all the world's birds took flight above them.

Everin tried to speak, but the ground shifted again, and her head swam.

Her mouth was still pulling in a gasp as she fell against the ground.

***

"What's going on?"

Everin's mouth tasted dry, and when her eyes snapped open, the world around them was moving.

She'd been slumped against Alaric's chest. Underneath them, Tracker galloped.

"They're after us again." Alaric's teeth were gritted, and his eyes flicked left and right, but Everin couldn't see them.

"What happened?"

Her memory blurred together. Had the ritual happened? Was this a part of it?

Her hand went to her face and came away wet. She looked down to see gleaming silver smudged into her skin, bright like moonlight.

"How'd they find us?" She couldn't get enough questions out.

Alaric's gold eyes moved away from her face. "You were screaming."

Something curdled in her stomach.

Tracker panted as branches scratched at their skin. Everin heard them at last, the shouts and sounds of their horses trampling the ground. Their enemies hadn't yet caught up to them, but there could be no mistake.

They were surrounded. The cacophony came from every direction.

She couldn't do this again. Her throat closed around the air inside it. She couldn't kill more of them. She wouldn't.

If the ritual worked, I might not be able to. There might not be enough of it left inside me for that.

Warm breath tickled her ear. "Can you do it again, silver-veined princess? Can you save these three lives?"

Everin couldn't think. There was unstifled emotion in his voice that would have been sacrilege to name. She silenced the thoughts clamoring inside her, begging to be acknowledged.

She twisted where she sat in front of Alaric. His quick breaths were on her cheek, and the world raced by faster than she could understand it.

Everin clamped her knees against Tracker and raised one open palm where she heard the hunters approaching fastest.

Silverblood, she spoke in her mind, calling to the fat snake coiled in her belly.

But the woods continued to race by, and their shouting was almost audible to her now. Everin nearly fell from Tracker in shock.

It was then that a streak of silver passed through the air from where her palm had been raised. It dissolved into something thinner than water vapor.

Her lips parted, and she felt even more lightheaded than when she'd woken.

"It's nearly gone," she said in a whisper.

Everin swallowed something down. It *had* worked.

She was almost normal again.

They were going to die.

The two thoughts collided in her simultaneously. This was to be her freedom and future, all at once.

And if she was going to die here, she wanted to enjoy it.

She only had to twist at her middle to do it. Everin's mouth was against his, tasting him.

If she pulled away now, she could claim it'd been an accident.

As his fingers tangled in her hair, she knew she couldn't go back. Heat rose from her belly and up into her throat. He took from her just as she had from him, tilting her head as she were a cup he drank from.

Alaric pulled away at last, clamping Everin to himself by their waists, and shoved his palm to the sky.

Something shot into the heavens like a meteor. Everin watched, unable to comprehend, as it fragmented into millions of pieces above their heads.

All the world went gray.

Her heart froze in her chest, and she scrambled to protect herself from the blast. Things like tree trunks broke around them. Other things did too, and she forced herself to listen.

Would this kill the three of them, too?

Her head pressed against Tracker as she clung to him. She didn't understand.

When the world quieted again, Everin lifted her head. Alaric had been knocked from Tracker, but he didn't look injured.

He looked ...

She banished the thought rattling inside her brain. Shaking, she dismounted from Tracker. To her relief, she found him uninjured when she ran her hands over his smooth sides.

She turned to the prince. "Are you hurt?"

Alaric's head snapped to her from where he'd been staring around him, speechless. When he looked at her then, she saw a glimpse of something behind his gold-veneer eyes.

It reminded her of when she'd seen a wildcat in the forests beyond the castle.

Never blinking. Focused. Hungry.

Don't be ridiculous. He's just in shock, like you.

Maybe more so than I am, she thought, remembering the kiss.

"I'm fine," he said at last as he came to his feet.

Her eyes couldn't stop moving. It was as if a harvest scythe of an unimaginable size had reaped the trees to their stumps.

How far did it go? Everin felt like fish were swimming inside her stomach. They needed to know.

"We should check that this hasn't reached a town. We should—"

Warm fingers clamped around her wrist. "We're running. Just as we always have. They're going to kill us for this."

Her pulse raged faster inside her veins. She couldn't stop thinking on it.

A settlement becomes a mile of gray, dead forest land.

Then it consumes a kingdom.

She pulled her hand away. She needed to think straight. She needed to see something green, blue, or brown again.

"How is this possible?" She didn't care how loud she was being anymore. The ones who had chased them were dead. Everything in hearing distance was dead. "Did the ritual not work? Did you know it wouldn't work?"

Even as she said it, she knew it was false. It had worked for her. What remained of her Silverblood was an echo of what had been there before.

She looked at him.

"How can you say that?" His voice was low. "I want this gone as much as you."

He stepped farther from her, and she hated the look he gave her then. She wanted more than anything for him not to look at her like that.

"I'm sorry—I know, but—" She shook her head, unable to continue. Tracker padded away from her, his gaze darting around the destruction, as if he couldn't believe what they'd done, either.

She closed her eyes. What had she meant?

"How far does this go?" she whispered.

Maybe we should have been caught, she thought. *Maybe this is worse.*

Nearby, Alaric was silent. Maybe there was no real answer to that.

Her fingers ran through her hair. "I'm sorry. I can't do this."

"Everin!"

But she'd already started running.

As the broken, withered trees fled past her, her breaths came faster. Her vision twisted, but still she ran. The deafening silence followed.

She needed to see that they hadn't killed every last thing here. She needed just a speck of life.

Something green. *Anything.*

A part of her knew she needed to be back with Tracker and Alaric—that more danger could be lurking in these deadened woods. But right now, she needed to know life existed still.

Her body couldn't seem to stop running.

Everin resolved to run until she never saw the color gray again. That was, until she saw her.

At first, her mind had taken the body to be another mage hunter. But her assumption didn't last long.

The body was much too frail. Her chest too unmoving. A basket of berries and herbs had been spilled some paces away.

The woman was curled against the gray ground like a quiet angel.

CHAPTER FIFTEEN

Everin woke among ashes and dust, her head still heavy against the ground. Her skin smudged with it as she wiped her face and blinked into a reluctant awareness.

She stared at her hands until she remembered how she'd gotten there.

After she'd seen what she'd seen in the woods, she'd kept running. She'd kept running even as men's shouts had soared through the air around her.

Even so, they hadn't found her. Her theory was that they were waiting in the bushes to kill her at her most unaware.

Prince Alaric and Tracker must have been driven in the opposite direction by the mage hunters. Or, at least, that's what she told herself.

The alternative was that they'd already killed them.

You need to find them. You need to know for sure.

But her legs had finally given up. Everin rubbed at a cut on her face to find out if her blood was red yet, but her hand was smeared with ash only.

Everin wished she could sleep away the woman in the woods, the shouts of the men hunting her, and the sight of her Silverblood.

But it was when she closed her eyes that she saw it all over again.

In her dreams, the woman's face had blended with her ma's. She couldn't dare sleep again.

No. Everin knew what she needed to do. She wouldn't leave again without putting her to rest.

Though she might not have been strong enough to bury her in the earth, Everin resolved to do what she could.

***

The sun's rays made fingers through the strange, half-mown woods. Hunger sapped strength from her, and Everin wavered on her feet. She slammed one hand against a still-standing tree to keep herself from falling.

She'd walked for much of the day without stopping. Even so, she had seen not one body—alive or otherwise.

At last, Everin gave up. She slumped to ground and pulled herself against the tree. Silent tears fell from her face to her collarbone.

What had they done?

Was surviving worth this?

The mage hunters are just as guilty, a voice inside her chimed. *They drove us to this.*

But what happened when the Silverblood emerged in her veins again from the incomplete ritual? What happened when the curse took her over entirely?

Then I become a monster, was the only answer loud enough to be heard in her mind.

As she sat in the quiet, she became slowly aware of something hanging in the tree above her.

It's our pack of supplies.

She stared at it in wonder. How had it missed being blasted apart in the attack? It felt like nothing short of a miracle.

Carefully, Everin started to climb. Several gray branches snapped to the ground, and she nearly fell more than once. Soon enough, however, she reached where their pack had been lodged and kept safe.

But her eyes went first to the sight below her. Knowing what the area had looked like a few days earlier made it all the worse.

From this vantage point, she could see all the destruction they'd brought here.

The valley forest they'd camped and ridden through was as empty as a dried canyon.

Stumps littered the area between half-downed trees. And everywhere was a fine film of ash and dust.

Just hours ago, a hungry woman had been picking food there. It had been her only crime.

Everin's grip nearly faltered.

Below, there was no sign of Alaric, Tracker, or even any mage hunters.

They left me behind here.

Maybe they thought me dead.

Maybe they wanted me dead.

She wasn't numb enough not to feel the sting of these possibilities, she realized with a jolt. The wind shifted her hair about her face, bringing the odd smell of Silver with it.

What was left to her now? Just a night ago, her thoughts had been markedly different.

The future had felt like a wide expanse. Now, there was only gray left.

Soon enough, her body's urges won out. Everin didn't move from the tree as she looked through their possessions for a morsel to keep her strength up.

But as the bag of their foraged berries tumbled into her fingers, Everin couldn't help but put them back.

She decided she wasn't hungry after all.

As she did so, Everin found the crumpled note she'd been fascinated by only a few days ago. It was the one that the strange bookseller had left for her without a word. The same one she'd studied all night just recently.

After a few moments, her eyes adjusted again to the letters, remembering their shapes and lines.

How trivial her desires from then seemed now. She'd wanted to practice reading to surprise Alaric with her ability after she was good enough with it. Or, rather, she'd wanted to seem more like his equal instead of the peasant girl he'd been stuck with because of their cursed blood.

She should have been watching for any sign of Alaric and Tracker from here, not indulging in her silly secret.

Everin almost put the note back in the bag when more crumpled paper fell out of it. She froze as her own face looked back up at her.

After the initial shock of seeing it passed, she remembered that she hadn't disposed of the threatening note like she'd intended. And there was another scrap of paper.

As soon as she flattened it, Everin recognized that it was the rest of the wanted notice. Words had been scrawled under her picture, likely ones warning other people that she was being hunted by the Guild and dangerous.

As the shadows of the day grew longer, Everin saw less and less sign of anyone or anything left alive in the area. Her heart grew heavier.

To distract herself as she watched for Alaric and to test her new skills, she started moving her gaze between the piece of paper the bookseller had given her, which had pictures next to words and had helped her understand some letters, and the wanted note.

Certain words were easy for her, such as *kill* and *red*, which both seemed to describe her. She frowned a little at her comically red hair in the picture but moved on.

Everin had once been quickly taught her letters, and she remembered from that time that the larger ones usually signified names of people or cities.

Her eyes caught on several after the word *kill*. Her stomach knotted when she realized the notice was telling people she'd killed the queen, king, Prince Adrian, and …

Her eyebrows came together. It had claimed she'd killed Alaric at the castle, too.

Everin felt as if her chest froze.

Although not the exact one, this note was the same kind as what she'd seen in the library that day.

Shortly after they'd left that place, the Guild's mage hunters had pursued them, yelling at her to release her prisoner.

Do they think I captured him?

Another thought struck her.

They think only I have Silverblood. They truly think I'm holding the prince captive.

It may have explained why the Guild captain had let them go the night of the fire festival. It also explained why she'd seen only her face on the wanted posters.

Everin closed her eyes. This meant that after the ritual, the prince would be able to reclaim his place among the royal family. He could claim he'd been captured by her rather than her co-conspirator as a Silverblood.

No one will have to know that he ever was one of us. No one will know he was ever infected with Silverblood.

Everin remembered their night together. The feeling of his touch on her skin. His soft kisses.

She vowed to keep it in her memory for good.

Because, after the ritual, she would disappear. She would leave and become a memory for Alaric.

Together, she and Tracker would make it on their own.

That's if they yet live, she considered.

Though these thoughts weren't comfortable, they gave her an odd sense of comfort.

But there was something still bothering her, and it rested in her hand. Why had the bookseller passed her the handwritten note at all? Why had he gone to such lengths to give her such a thing?

"You can't read, can you?"

She knew now, or suspected, that this had been his way of trying to teach her to read. But why would this bookseller she'd never met care about that?

Other than to sell more books, she snorted to herself.

It still didn't make sense to her. Unless ...

He'd been trying to tell her something through showing her how to read. Everin studied the note but only saw a list of letters, common words, and their corresponding pictures.

Does this have to do with the Book of Dissimulation?

Was he trying to tell me to read it?

As Everin stared beyond the barren valley, she considered two things. First, she needed to make sure she would never hurt anyone else with the magic in her veins. And second ...

There's more than a ritual in that book, she thought. *But why should I trust this bookseller?*

And then there was the counter: *Perhaps because he could have had me killed or captured when I was there.*

He knew what I was.

It occurred to her in the same moment that she saw two riders nearly fly down the side of the valley towards its bottom.

Even from this distance, Everin could see that one horse bore an uncanny resemblance to her closest friend.

Tracker.

And, under the thick cloak he wore, his rider had to be Alaric.

Her gaze went to the rider after him. Tracker had outpaced their hunter for now, but it wouldn't be long until they collided again.

And what had happened would happen again. A face flashed in her mind.

This is because of me. They think I'm the only one with Silverblood.

What happens when the Silver kills him this time? Or Tracker?

She barely had the time before Alaric was forced to defend himself and he would be forced to expose the curse in his veins, so she worked without thinking.

When her hand dug into their bag, she found what she'd wanted. Everin put the swan mask on her face after tying her hair back. Before she jumped out of the tree, she hesitated just a moment.

A few lines of ash smudged her cheeks like war paint.

Now that she looked the part of the villain, all that was left to do was act it out.

She would be using a different type of weapon than cursed magic.

CHAPTER SIXTEEN

Luckily for Prince Aleksander, his mount's hooves barely trod the ground as they raced.

It was as if the beast was afraid of the earth itself.

All around him, trees had been blanched a dead gray color. More were scattered across the ground in splinters big enough to spear through several men clean like a kabob.

This was perhaps the first time he'd seen what it could do up close, and it was worse than he could've imagined.

Aleksander refused to call it a body recovery search. Even if the Guild had given up on finding Alaric, he wouldn't.

His father's advisors and the Guild would have called what he was doing too dangerous. Which was exactly why they didn't know he was doing this.

But no one else had caught her so far. And Aleksander didn't believe that she was dead, as the Guild hoped.

Not when Vaun had slipped him some information: their Silverblood detection meters were showing slightly higher than normal readings in the area still. It was odd considering it was much lower than one might expect from a living, breathing Silverblood. The Guild claimed it was just residual, as if from her corpse, but Aleksander knew better.

He'd found evidence of her here. Lingering and very alive.

His knight, Oren, had taken the southern perimeter. He hadn't told Oren that the readings were strongest on the other side of the woods because Aleksander needed to do this himself. He would kill this girl by day's end.

And he'd picked up on her trail just before the sun had started to set.

His grip tightened on the reins of his horse. Aleksander remembered well how he'd found her supplies left alone that day. In return, he'd left her a friendly note expressing his intentions.

After Vaun had told him that his brother truly lived, he hadn't been able to sleep. He would bring his family's murderer to justice.

He'd end this nightmare for good.

He routed his horse along the edge of the valley where they had the cover of the dead trees. Beyond them stretched a sea of their stubs.

Aleksander cursed under his breath. He'd lost her.

Or had he?

The fear began as a cold, slow slug in his belly. A silent wind stirred the dust around him.

It would only take an instant. A gray flash perhaps, and then he would feel nothing more.

Aleksander pulled free one of his swords and held it low against his horse's side. His eyes flashed to each side of the clearing. Where would've he waited to ambush his enemy?

I have to assume she doesn't know my exact position and that I'm too close to her for her to safely blast me into pieces.

Aleksander headed for the most obvious hiding spot, a tight gathering of trees that remained tall enough to climb, aimed and threw his sword for the second obvious spot, and tucked his head in as he jumped from his horse.

His world was a mesh of sky, earth, and unending gray. On the ground, he wasted no time as he pulled himself as upright as possible and freed another of his swords from a sheath.

The wreckage around him had turned from a silent grave to a strange cacophony. Though no flock of birds took to the air as he'd have expected in a living forest, pieces of branches and dead detritus broke around his fall, piercing the dull quiet.

His horse protested his sudden departure though he didn't deviate from the path Aleksander had set him on, circling the thicket when he arrived at it. Nothing came from within the broken trees.

Where his sword had hit was another matter entirely.

His blade barely missed her face, lodging itself deep in the trunk of the tree above where she emerged.

Aleksander rounded on her, another sword already in his hands.

Her face was wild. She wore a festival mask with glimmering white gems that mocked him. Gray ash was smeared across her cheeks like war paint.

It was the first time he'd seen his family's killer in the flesh, and she seemed about as sane as he'd assumed.

Aleksander was about to charge her and put his blade through her heart when he saw him.

He'd been so arrested by the sight of her that he hadn't seen who she'd brought with her out of her hiding spot.

Alaric.

It was like seeing a ghost.

His younger brother's dark hair was mussed and littered with pieces of ash. His eyes were almost as wild as the Silverblood's.

Aleksander didn't breathe. He didn't think he could.

At Alaric's throat, the Silverblood pushed a long knife. His hands were behind his back as if bound.

"Don't," she said between a swallow. "Or else."

Aleksander's blood thundered. He would free him.

"Hurt him, and you're done," Aleksander vowed. "Release him now."

But his words were a lie. She was done no matter what. He would kill her for this.

"No. You're letting me go," she said. His eyes caught on the Silverblood's other hand which held a pool of Silver.

His pulse ran hot through him. He would free him.

"You wouldn't kill yourself, too," he said through his teeth. "Even a monster has self-preservation."

Her dark brown eyes seemed to widen and catch on that he was talking about her.

Good.

"And you wouldn't risk him," she said in a similar gasp through her teeth.

The problem was that she was right. It was then that he saw her eyes catch on his royal clothes. They moved until she looked straight into his face as she'd avoided doing so far.

She didn't realize who I was before, he thought with a jolt.

It would be his opening. He would free his brother from this Silverblood if it was the last thing he did.

Aleksander had almost no time. From his years of practice at the knight academy, he knew how to move in those seconds to get what he wanted.

He had to end this Silverblood utterly. He had to stab her through the heart with one thrust.

It was a tall order, but he'd done it before.

She was still in a state of surprise when he twisted his arm faster than the flight of a bird. She wouldn't get away this time.

But it seemed like another force pulled his brother closer, over her heart. The movement jostled the knife closer to Alaric, and a bit of the Silverblood she held spilled across his front. Aleksander pulled back from his strike almost too late.

Alaric should have been recoiling from the burn of the silver on his skin, but he seemed to be holding the pain back to speak.

"Aleksander," he said through a clenched jaw. "Leave me. Now."

He stared at his brother. "I'm not going to. I would never leave you to a monster." His breaths came harder.

"Stay away, Aleksander. Far away." Something tightened in Alaric's gaze. "You'll end up killing me if you follow. And yourself."

Aleksander faltered, trying to understand the words.

It was all the opening that the Silverblood needed in order to take his brother deeper in the cursed wood.

CHAPTER SEVENTEEN

"You were magnificent." Alaric held his mouth near her ear. His breath rose bumps across her skin.

Everin couldn't understand how she was still alive. She was shaking too badly to hold to Tracker's reins. Alaric must have noticed because he shifted his hands over hers.

In the short moments during which she'd intercepted Alaric and Tracker and explained her plan, Everin had bargained on fooling a Guild captain with their fake hostage scheme. Not this.

"Did you know it was him following you? Did you know it was your brother?" Her words came out in a gasp.

Alaric pulled her closer. Her heartbeat raced against the feeling of his skin.

"I had my suspicions. But I wasn't sure," he said under his breath. She felt his fists tighten. "But I'm *glad* it was him. It's good that he doesn't realize what I am."

"That was worse than facing one of the hunters," Everin blurted. She felt lost. Why hadn't he told her?

"If I'd have told you it was him, would you have performed so well?" he asked.

The answer, she knew, was no. But only because she wouldn't have attempted it at all.

What's important is that it worked, she considered.

But now that she'd lied to the prince who would likely be crowned king soon, what would happen to her?

When she'd found Alaric, Everin had explained her hunch that the Guild thought only she possessed Silverblood magic.

And yet, she hadn't told him that she'd figured that detail out by learning to read. For some reason, it felt childish now that she'd spent those hours not trying to find him and Tracker or even the woman in the woods, but sitting and reading.

"No, I wouldn't have," she said finally. "But how can you be sure it worked?"

"Because you were good enough to nearly fool me," he said. His golden eyes were dark when they moved to her face.

She let the words settle within her. Whether they were successful or not at their ruse, only time would tell.

For now, as the darkness chased at their heels through the deadened wood, there was another matter to sort out.

Everin's voice was low. "We have to find her before we leave the area."

Alaric was silent.

She continued. "She needs to be buried."

When Alaric said nothing yet again, Everin moved to retake control over Tracker's reins. On horseback, they could cover a much wider area.

And, if she'd done as good of a job as Alaric said, then they had nothing to worry about for now.

"Everin, no." His voice was just as low as hers though much firmer.

Her voice became more unsteady the longer she spoke. "She needs our help. We did that, Alaric."

But his hands were like iron on hers, keeping their trajectory straight ahead.

His voice was too quiet when he spoke. "We go back for her, and they find us. We won't live to bury her. We need to ride to the location of the last page first. We need to do this."

In her heart, she knew he was right. But that didn't make her feel it was right to leave her behind like that.

All she could see was the woman's empty expression, over and over in her mind.

I'll be back. I'll bury you.

"Okay," she whispered finally. She needed to get her mind off what she'd seen in the woods, so she pulled out what had been one of the many thoughts from her mind's storm. "Are you sure you know where the last page is hidden?"

When she'd met with Alaric, one of the first things he'd told her was that he'd found where the last page of the ritual was, though he hadn't ventured there yet to verify it.

But Everin couldn't help but resist hope. After all, how many towns and cities had they combed? How many libraries and bookshops had turned out to be wastes of time?

She would believe it when she saw it.

Alaric stared straight ahead, though the corner of his lip pulled up in a smirk. "No, but I have a strong hunch."

"We've travelled through all the notable towns. We narrowly escaped the cities. Where else is there besides the Guild's head-quarters?" she thought out loud.

Her stomach churned. *Not there. Anywhere but there.*

"Good guess, but no," Alaric said. "We haven't found it because it's something that was torn out of the book and left at the castle."

Everin's stomach sank.

"The castle ... as in the one that the Guild burnt," she said. *It will be a pile of ashes now.*

But Alaric didn't seem discouraged. Instead, his gaze shot forward with an odd look in his eyes. Like he could see exactly where the page was before him. He leaned forward, and Tracker moved faster.

"That's just it. It's been protected from fire. Protected from sight." Alaric's gaze didn't waver from the invisible specter before him. "There is a layer of hollowed stone in my father's study that he thought no one else knew about."

"Why do you think it's there?" Everin heard herself ask. "And why now?"

"He ... suspected what I was. It's the last place it could be." It was all Alaric seemed able to say.

"Alright. We have to try. We have to find it," she said.

It was one of the two things she'd resolved to do after losing touch with Alaric. Her second goal came to mind then.

She needed to find out what was written on the book's pages. Everin needed to puzzle out the mystery of the bookseller's strange behavior.

"Alaric. I wanted to ask something about that," she started. "What ... exactly is on those pages?"

The prince didn't react like how she'd thought he would. A smile quirked to his lips, though his eyes remained on the path before them.

"Worried we don't have the supplies? I took care of it all while finding you, my love." His smile dissolved. "Between my manic searching."

Before she could add anything, his hand was on her chin. "Speaking of that." Alaric moved her head to look at him. "When I thought I'd lost you ... Those were the worst moments of my life. Never."

He breathed and closed his eyes for a second. "Never do that again."

"I'm sorry, Alaric." Everin's cheeks felt scorching hot. She could've stopped there. Should've, maybe. But the words tumbled forward.

"But you don't really mean that ... for *after*. We'll be cured of the cursed magic and leave each other. We have to. You'll be a prince and I'll be a—"

"The wife of one," Alaric said. His gaze was intense, all hint of his usual mischief gone. "If you'd have him."

"Alaric." Her voice was tight, and she felt dizzy. He didn't mean that ... did he? "I couldn't."

"You could."

From his pockets, he fished out the beautiful earrings of his mother's. He fixed them on each of her ears before kissing her neck.

As they rode through the wood to find the world colorful again, her eyes ached from the color. After the gray, seeing everything so in bloom around her almost felt like a fairy tale.

But in her heart's core, she knew there was something in the pages of that book that she needed to see.

Something Alaric didn't know about.

Or something he doesn't want me to know about.

The thought was quiet, like a whisper, as the cold gems tickled her neck.

CHAPTER EIGHTEEN

The castle wasn't as she'd remembered it.

The stone parts of it remained like a skeleton watching them approach. The rest had been reduced to odd piles of rubble and ash.

Everin and Alaric rode onto its grounds with a silence that followed them like shadows of the too-bright day.

They left Tracker by the river that flowed by its boundaries. Alaric had dipped two of their canteens inside it as Everin had bade him to be a good boy in their absence. Everin didn't look at where the stables used to be.

As they walked into the empty courtyard, Everin trembled for those that had died here.

"Are you sure you're ready for this?" Alaric asked before they stepped inside the grand doors. His eyes were bright like the sun above them.

It was the question she'd been asking herself all the way here. No matter what she suspected was written on the last page of the Book of Dissimulation, Everin needed to go forward to find it.

Even if she had a plan to discover its contents before then.

She nodded, and Alaric shifted so he was before her. In one of his hands was their knife, poised to break his skin to release the Silverblood inside if necessary. The other pulled open the door.

Everin wasn't sure what she'd been expecting.

The bodies of servants left behind to die. A room full of Guild mage hunters. The castle main hall as it had been before the Guild's attack.

Instead of any of that, it was empty except for more rubble and ash staining the walls. As they came to the stairwell that Alaric said led to his father's study, he cursed under his breath.

A metal beam had fallen before it, blocking their progress.

"I should be able to move it, but it will take a few minutes," he said.

As he started to move the burnt detritus at the base of the stairs, Everin came to the window that afforded her a view of what had been the castle gardens.

A thin swirl of smoke was barely visible against the bright sky some distance away.

It was in the direction they'd come from.

It could be a chimney fire from the village not far from here.

It could be a traveler's campfire. Or even the Guild's harmless fire as they stop for the day.

But in this hall that they had burnt down to hunt them before, Everin didn't like the look of it.

She needed to get to the book.

Everin came to Alaric's side. He'd nearly cleared the beam out of the way.

"I'll take the pack while you do that," she said.

But before she could slip it off his shoulder, he shrugged it away from her. "No need. We're going up now."

He waved her ahead as a gentleman would, though her stomach pinched. He took her hand in his to steady her and lead her up the stairs.

When they walked into dead King Nikhil's study, Everin felt that this had been a sanctuary before. Wide windows stretched the expanse of one side, offering an unobstructed view of the countryside.

The skeletons of furniture had been pushed against the walls. In one corner was a bed and a dark black burnt spot underneath it.

Her eyes turned away from that corner.

On a bench near the middle of the room that was almost entirely intact, Alaric pulled free several materials: his knife, their canteens of water, and some bandages. Everin pretended not to watch as she inspected what she could of the walls.

But Alaric kept the pack with the rest of the supplies—most importantly, the book—still on his shoulder.

"What are we searching for?" she asked out loud. She'd approached the wall as well as she could, but there was even more burnt rubble here than had been downstairs.

Alaric was by her side at once. He took her hand in his and moved them to the stone.

"Check any mark on the wall. Anywhere it looks like a stone has been slid out before," Alaric said.

He released her hand, and she moved hers across the cold stone. "How did you ever find this?" she wondered out loud, but her voice only echoed softly against the hard surface.

When she turned her head, she saw he was gone, likely to search the other half of the room.

It wasn't the only strange behavior that she'd observed in him, however. Something in his demeanor had bothered her when they'd arrived on the burnt castle grounds.

As she considered what it was, her eyes went to the wide view next to her out the study's windows.

Everin stopped. The clouds of smoke were bigger than only moments before.

And, more importantly, closer.

They were coming for them. There was no doubt.

No.

They're coming for me.

Her pulse pounded through her veins. Something was wrong here.

Something had always been wrong with this.

"Alaric." The word scratched out of her throat like a whisper.

When she turned, he wasn't searching the walls at all. He had in his hand the Book of Dissimulation. In his other was the only knife they had left.

His eyes were already on hers. "I suspected they'd follow us. We might have stopped Aleksander, but the Guild could never be placated. Not until they see red from your veins." His hand that held the knife motioned her towards him. "Here, my love. We're performing the ritual here."

She stared at the book. Her time was up.

"You found the other page?" Her voice was too weak.

He glanced at her, once, before washing the edge of the knife in one of their canteens.

"Everything we need is here. I have it all ready for you."

She didn't miss how he hadn't answered. Her eyes fell on the bed in the corner.

There was never a second page.

What does it mean? Why are we here?

"It will take it away, Everin. I promise."

Everin felt herself walk forward. He'd placed the opened book on the table, a single torn page against its bared spine.

Closer, and she could possibly read it. Maybe.

Everin thrust her hands out. "Can I help?"

Prince Alaric's palm was against her face, stroking her cheek. "There's nothing to fear, my love."

"I know there's not." Everin tried and failed to suppress a shiver. His golden eyes unfocused her like strong drink. "But I'd feel better if I helped this time."

"Do you trust me?" Alaric said.

It was the same question he'd asked her before the first ritual.

She didn't hear him. Her eyes were on the top of the torn page. It was the first time since she'd started to read that she had seen it.

The embossed letters were in an older style, embellished with unnecessary flourishes that made her familiar letters look alien. Difficult to read.

But not impossible.

For the first time, she started to understand. This wasn't the spell she'd thought it was.

"Everin?"

At her name, she started. In his hands were not only the book, but the only weapon between them. And she only had enough Silverblood in her veins to get killed for it.

Everin made a decision, even as her mouth said something else entirely.

"Of course, I do."

Thoughts raced from her like water from a cracked pot. She had to make a plan, here and now. She knew too much.

Her eyes were still on the book, but she didn't think he'd noticed. She had to get the weapon in her hands. Everything would be better, then.

He took the knife in his dominant hand as he drew apart the strings of his tunic at his throat.

Alaric offered her a smile that slowly reached the edges of his mouth. He looked how nameless, coinless boys had smiled at her before.

She wished that was all he was.

Her heart raced as he pushed the cotton from his bare skin. His chest was as beautiful as the rest of him with smooth skin quivering with his own heartbeat.

"I'll do it first to show you," he said. "We'll need to speak the words in the book to start the incantation. Fortunately, I've memorized that part, so you'll repeat them after me."

Everin wasn't satisfied, but she smiled back. The prince was lying to her, and she didn't know why yet. She needed more time.

"What about the knife?" she wondered out loud. She swallowed, letting some of her anxiety seep through. "Last time ..."

Alaric nodded. "You're right. I'll need to make a cut on each of us again. But I'll try to make it as painless and shallow as possible."

"You'll show me first?"

Alaric smiled at her question. "Yes. Just repeat the words after me." The prince started, "I call on that which was given to me so I may offer thanks."

Everin's mouth repeated the phrase verbatim. The problem was, these were not the words written in the book below.

The facts squatted in her mind as a goblin would've. Unwanted. Undeniable.

She had to buy time. She had to understand what the words at her fingers said.

"You can't read, can you?"

The bookseller hadn't been mocking her. He'd been trying to teach her to read. He'd wanted her to know something.

"What's wrong?"

At the sound of Alaric's voice, she realized she hadn't repeated the next phrase he'd fed her. She hadn't even heard what he meant her to repeat this time.

She floundered for what to say. "It's a lot of words to remember."

"It is," he agreed. "Fewer at once, then."

She peeked at the text in her hands while he was distracted. There was one word that repeated over and over.

"I give what has been given," Alaric said.

She recited the phrase, only sparing a glimpse at the real words in the book below. There were so many of them, and none of the ones she knew helped her.

"And conceal this part of me," he said.

"And conceal this part of me," she repeated.

As she spoke, her eyes caught on a word she did know.

Steal.

Her heart skipped several beats. He brought the knife out again, allowing the weak sunlight from the windows to glint off the smooth metal. "That completes this part."

She'd lost. There was no more time. Everin didn't know his intention or what this ritual was calling upon.

Think! What do you know?

What she knew was she was utterly alone with Prince Alaric. He'd proven that to her already. She knew that he held their only weapon, and Silverblood ran strong in his veins.

Everin bit the tip of her tongue. Those thoughts hadn't helped except to show her how much power over her the prince had now.

You know that the last ritual worked.

But that wasn't quite true, was it?

She frowned. Her Silverblood had nearly left her, but the same couldn't have been said for the prince.

Maybe it worked—but not for the reason you think.

A thought sparked inside her. As he waited wordlessly on her, she managed to speak. "Show me what to do next. Without pain," she added.

"As you wish," Prince Alaric said.

He turned the sharp edge towards him. It was all Everin saw before she averted her eyes to the open text between them.

Wherever he was cutting on his skin, he was sure to take care doing it. It wouldn't afford her much time, but it was the best she had.

Silently, Everin mouthed out the words, stopping as she came to the one that had confounded her from the start. She pieced together the sounds.

She stared at the sentence at her fingers. It was all she could do.

"In order to fully transfer the power of Silverblood to oneself, a final sacrifice is necessary."

Her head was dizzy. She read it over again, but the meaning didn't change. It stared back at her, dully.

It was the smell that first alerted her. Silverblood was in the air, stronger than before.

Everin's head darted up. She fought to control her expression, but she felt she'd lost the battle.

Prince Alaric had been watching her the entire time.

Words bubbled to her lips, but he spoke first. "Are you ready? I'll do yours for you."

A shallow cut was carved below his throat. One corner of it dribbled a thin line of silver.

Her Silverblood.

He'd never possessed Silverblood, not any of his own.

The word waited on her tongue, unspoken like a weapon. But even as she nearly spoke it aloud, she remembered the wisp she'd managed when the mage hunters had been pursuing them.

And the blast that he'd managed.

There was little doubt in her mind that she shouldn't allow him near her with the blade. As if she were dreaming, she couldn't move as he approached her. Drops of silver fell to the floor from the steel.

His fingers were at the base of her throat where her heart lodged. They paused, poised at the first button of her shirt.

"What do these words mean?" she breathed into his face.

"I'll teach you after." He cupped her face in one of his hands, one thumb running across her lower lip. His other hand held the knife, hovering over her skin.

His thumb was still on her lip as she said, "I thought losing all that would give you nightmares."

The world seemed to slow as she continued, "But you sleep so soundly."

Her eyes flickered to the page one last time. The letters flowed as words through her mind.

"In the house of Death, kill the subject with the knife blessed by river water."

There was enough time to grab the hilt of the weapon and angle it away from her. But she couldn't free it from his grasp.

She felt it before she saw it. The sound of the slap reverberated against the stone walls surrounding them. Pain stung her cheek and tears clouded her vision, but she couldn't let go.

"I will do worse," the prince snarled. "Release the knife."

She didn't bother responding as she dug an elbow into his stomach. The pressure at her wrist grew to an unbearable degree as he squeezed. She released the hilt of the knife with a sharp gasp.

Her chest heaved at her defeat.

Everin was strong, but Alaric had been stronger.

"I will be the first Silverblood king. It's my destiny, Everin." The look in his eyes captured hers. With every ounce of his being, he believed it.

"You're out of your mind," she breathed. But he only smiled at that.

He circled her now, the knife still coated in Silverblood as he held it low. Abruptly, he stopped. His expression was still that of the boyish prince who had shared her quilt. "Come, and I'll make it quick. Painless. Run, and I can't promise that," he said.

Everin took one step. And then another. It was the only path before her. She was within arm's distance of him when she spoke.

"Did Queen Roen beg for mercy when her youngest son killed her? Did King Nikhil fight when his last heir killed him in his sleep?"

It had been a guess, and a guess was a poor thing to stake a life on. But it was enough.

The knife slid from his slack fingers and into hers. She dodged his retaliation in the same second while gripping the knife and aiming for him. But what he did next froze her.

His fingers were smeared in the silver from his chest. He'd raised his palm in warning.

"I will kill us both with it," Alaric promised, "and everything around us."

Breath left her lungs.

Before she spoke, she hadn't known the truth of it. But her words stirred something in her belly, solid and hungry.

"You can't hurt me with what's mine."

And she opened his throat, spilling silver until only red was left.

EPILOGUE

He should have never let her go.

It was all that was on Aleksander's mind as he rode through the charred woods where a Silverblood had taken his brother to kill him.

His hands tightened on his horse's reins. Vaun had said, despite his warning, the Guild's leader had ordered a fire cleansing of the woods.

Did it tip her off?

Did it push her hand?

But he'd never know now whether the Guild's actions had exacerbated the situation or not. Even so, he couldn't help his suspicions.

It's almost like Marka wanted him dead, too.

Ahead of him, Vaun raised his fist to stop their party. At once, his High Knight Oren sidled up next to him to better protect him.

Aleksander's breath fogged in the gray morning. "Is it her?" It was the only question that mattered.

He'd too long hoped they'd find some sign of her self-destruction. According to Vaun, it happened far less than one would hope, but Silverbloods did occasionally take care of themselves.

Whether by the madness in their veins or by accident, Aleksander wasn't all that interested in finding out.

But Vaun's head shook. "No sign of her still, according to my meter. My eyes caught on these, though. Are they familiar to you?"

His friend passed a bundle to him. In his palm were two brilliant diamond earrings. Their metal was cold to his skin, and Aleksander closed his hand over them.

There was no doubt to him who they'd once belonged to. Or what she'd intended, leaving them here like trash in her path, probably torn from her ears with blood-stained hands.

For this, too, the girl would pay.

His Silverblood monster.

Also by Joy Lewis

A Dance of Gilded Lies (Silverblood Series Book 2)

* * *

A Thorn among Fae (Fae Crown Book 1)
A Crown for the Cursed (Fae Crown Book 2)
The War of the Wicked (Fae Crown Book 3)

* * *

The Lost Princess (A Sleeping Beauty Retelling)

* * *

Wither Thorn (The Crest of Blackthorn Book 1)
Soul Sworn (The Crest of Blackthorn Book 2)
Marrow Blade (The Crest of Blackthorn Book 3)
Blood Prophecy (The Crest of Blackthorn Book 4)
Heir of Thorns (A Crest of Blackthorn Prequel)

ACKNOWLEDGEMENTS

I'd like to first thank you, the reader, for coming on this journey with me, and special thanks to my newsletter readers in particular. I couldn't have written this without their feedback on the first version of this story.

Of course, I couldn't release a book without thanking Roman Smith. Thank you for our compulsory walks in the morning (my doing) and for our compulsory wind-downs at night (your doing). Thank you for your support through both the storm and the calm.

Thank you to Laura Bell-Seibers, Ashlie Bell-Seibers, Lake House-McCoig, and Fern House-McCoig for the laughs, excellent food, and even better company. Please come over more—there is far too much food here.

About the Author

From the time she "borrowed" a floppy disk from her school's computer lab at the age of 12 to type her first story, Joy Lewis has been dreaming up tales of adventure and danger for most of her life. In 2017, she graduated with highest distinction from Middle Tennessee State University with a B.A. in English. She lives in Tennessee where she can be found in her garden when not writing.

Sign up for her newsletter for a free book at www.joylewis author.com.